DOCTOR WHO AND THE
MONSTER OF PELADON

DOCTOR WHO AND THE MONSTER OF PELADON

Based on the BBC television serial by Brian Hayles by arrangement with the British Broadcasting Corporation

TERRANCE DICKS

A TARGET BOOK
published by
the Paperback Division of
W. H. Allen & Co. Ltd.

A Target Book
Published in 1980
By the Paperback Division of W. H. Allen & Co. Ltd
A Howard & Wyndham Company
44 Hill Street, London W1X 8LB

ISBN 0 426 20132 9

Made and printed in Great Britain by
The Anchor Press Ltd, Tiptree, Essex

Contents

1

Return to Peladon

On the remote edges of the galaxy was a planet called Peladon. It was a bleak and mountainous place, lashed by howling storms, lit at night by the fierce blaze of three moons. A primitive, barbarous world, inhabited by warriors, hunters, and savage beasts, fierce bear-like creatures with tusks and one mighty horn, who roamed the wooded slopes of the high mountains.

The warriors of Peladon both hunted and worshipped the beast called Aggedor. No young Peladonian was reckoned truly a man until he had slain one in single combat. Because of its strength and valour, Aggedor became the sacred symbol of the Royal House of Peladon. Unfortunately, it also became very nearly extinct.

Time brought other changes. Under a young and progressive king, Peladon joined the Galactic Federation, allying itself with other more civilised planets.

The alliance was not accomplished without difficulty. Hepesh, High Priest of Peladon clung fiercely to the old ways, rebelling against his king and combining with a treacherous Federation delegate called Arcturus to keep Peladon isolated. The plot was foiled by a wandering Time Lord called the Doctor. He arrived on Peladon apparently by chance, was mistaken for a Federation delegate, and later vanished as mysteriously as he had come.

Time passed, and King Peladon was succeeded by his daughter. The Galactic Federation became embroiled in war with Galaxy Five, and suddenly Peladon was a planet of vital strategic importance. The mountains and rocks of Peladon were rich in trisilicate, a mineral vital to the war effort.

Now more intensive mining began, and Federation technicians were brought in to speed up the process.

The war with Galaxy Five dragged Peladon towards a technological future with brutal speed. Clashes between the old ways and the new were inevitable, and once again there were rumblings of mutiny from the more traditionally minded Peladonians. Was this all the benefit of joining the Federation—more toil in the mines, now under alien overseers?

Affairs on Peladon were moving towards a crisis. Then the Doctor reappeared . . .

A little party of miners toiled through an immense cavern deep in the heart of Mount Megashra, sacred mountain of Peladon. They wore rough working-clothes, and their hands and faces were grained deep with trisilicate dust. The cathedral-like cavern was the meeting point of many tunnels and mine galleries, and its strangely twisted stalagmites and stalactites gave a weird subterranean beauty to the scene.

Between them the miners trundled a sonic lance, a device like a small wheeled cannon, newly introduced into the mining operation. Ettis, the squad leader harried them along, a thin, wiry young man, sharp-featured and sharp-voiced.

'Come on, come on, keep it moving. Mustn't keep our lords and masters waiting.' He pointed to a tunnel directly ahead. 'Straight down there.'

Suddenly a glowing spot appeared on the cavern wall. With terrifying speed it grew into a blazing corona of light, and in the heart of the fireball appeared a familiar and terrifying form.

The miners staggered back, before the blast of heat, covering their eyes and bowing their heads in fear.

A ray of light sped from the heart of the apparition. It touched one of the miners, his body glowed brightly, and he screamed once and vanished. His fellows turned and fled in terror. Behind them the glowing apparition faded from the cavern wall.

In a tunnel not far away, two relative newcomers to Peladon were engaged in an earnest technical discussion. One was called Vega Nexos, a mole-man from the planet Vega. Most of the inhabitants of Vega lived in tunnels of one kind or another, and the Vegans were famous mining engineers, who sold their skills all over the galaxy. The second was an Earthman called Eckersley, a tall, lean man with a wry, sardonic face. Like Vega Nexos, he was a mining engineer. Both wore light silver cover-alls—the badge of the technician throughout the galaxy.

Eckersley was brandishing a chunk of rock, shot through with gleaming metallic veins. 'I agree, the quality's marvellous—but we're not even producing *enough* to refine yet.'

Vega Nexos gave a snort of discontent. 'How can we, when these primitives cling to their picks and shovels? We bring modern equipment here and they refuse to let us use it.'

'Oh, they'll come round in time,' said Eckersley tolerantly. 'At least they agreed to try out the sonic lance.'

There were yells from down the tunnel, and the sound of rushing feet. A group of terrified miners rounded a bend in the tunnel, shot past them and ran on.

Eckersley reached out a long arm and grabbed the last

of the group, forcing him to a halt. 'Hey, Ettis, what's going on? What's all the panic?'

'It is Aggedor! We brought the sonic cannon as you ordered and the spirit of Aggedor appeared and slew one of us for blasphemy.' Ettis wrenched himself free. 'Do you think anyone will use your alien equipment now, Earthman?'

Before Eckersley could reply, Ettis had followed the others down the tunnel.

In the throne room of the Citadel of Peladon, the great castle on the peak of the sacred mountain, a meeting was held to discuss the crisis.

The huge stone-walled chamber was richly draped with hanging tapestries. Torches flared smokily in holders formed in the shape of the snarling face of Aggedor.

At the end of the great hall on a raised dais was the great ceremonial throne, now occupied by the slender figure of Queen Thalira. A frail and beautiful girl, still very young, she seemed almost crushed by the weight of her crown and ceremonial jewels. Behind her towered the massive figure of Blor, the Queen's Champion, powerful arms folded over his mighty chest. At the Queen's right hand, a little behind the throne, stood Ortron, who was both Chancellor and High Priest. An ornately robed, impressively bearded figure, he was the Queen's chief adviser and the holder of the real power on Peladon.

A strangely assorted group was assembled before the throne. At the centre were the two engineers, Eckersley and Vega Nexos. Beside them stood Alpha Centauri, Ambassador of the Galactic Federation. To the Peladonians, unused to the infinite variety of intelligent lifeforms, his was an extraordinary figure. The body was a single column, draped in a cloak emblazoned with the insignia of a Federation Ambassador. The head was octopoid with a single enormous eye. Six rippling tentacles projected from beneath the cloak. They waved and stirred continuously, like branches in the breeze, reflecting every shade of Alpha Centauri's feelings. For all his rather intimidating appearance, Alpha Centauri was a gentle and sensitive creature. He was finding the position of Federation Ambassador on a primitive and strife-torn planet a considerable strain on his delicate sensibilities.

Chancellor Ortron surveyed the motley group with disfavour. He was no lover of aliens, however politically distinguished or technically qualified. His glare settled on Eckersley. 'One of our miners has been killed, the others are terrified and refuse to work. Explain!'

Eckersley had worked on a lot of planets and it took more than an angry Chancellor to intimidate him. 'Not up to me to explain, is it? The miners say it was the spirit of Aggedor, whatever that means.'

'Do not blaspheme, alien,' rumbled Ortron.

Alpha Centauri said 'I am sure no disrespect was intended, Chancellor.' His voice was high-pitched and twittering, a fitting expression of his nervous temperament.

In his low grunting voice, Vega Nexos said, 'I am a practical engineer. I find it difficult to accept that this incident was brought about by supernatural means.'

'Then what is your explanation?'

'Sabotage.'

'And who are these saboteurs?'

Eckersley said, 'Saboteurs or spooks, the result's the same. Your miners are refusing to use the sonic gun.'

Queen Thalira spoke for the first time. 'The use of this sonic cannon is essential to you?'

Eckersley shrugged. 'It will increase output tenfold, Your Majesty. Save your miners a lot of hard work with pick and shovel.'

'Then arrange an immediate demonstration. If our people see that we have faith in the new technology, it may calm their fears.'

Alpha Centauri's tentacles rippled as he inclined forward in a bow. 'Allow me to thank Your Majesty on behalf of the Federation.'

Thalira raised her hand. 'Thank you, Ambassador. The audience is at an end.'

The aliens left in a group, and Ortron leaned closer to the throne, dominating the Queen with his bulk. 'I must protest, Your Majesty. To expose yourself to danger . . .'

'You know as well as I, Ortron, that it was my father's dream to see Peladon a member of the Federation. He signed the treaty, and now I must honour it—even if it means my people must make sacrifices in a quarrel not their own.' Queen Thalira sighed. 'We must accept the duties of Federation membership, Ortron, as well as its privileges.'

Ortron bowed, 'I shall go to the temple, Your Majesty, and seek guidance from the spirit of Aggedor.'

In one of the tunnels just beneath the Citadel, a guard on routine patrol was astonished to hear a strange wheezing, groaning noise and even more astonished to see a square blue box appearing out of thin air. Strange rumours of terrifying events in the mines below had been circulating through the Citadel, and overcome with superstitious terror, he turned and fled.

Since he was a brave and conscientious man despite his fear, he stopped at a bend in the tunnel keeping the box under observation from a safe distance.

He was amazed to see its door open and a tall white-haired man in strange clothes step out, followed by a female alien, equally strangely dressed.

The Doctor looked around him and rubbed his chin.

'Well, according to my calculations, Sarah, we should be in the Citadel of Peladon, one of the most impressive sights—'

'Well, we're not, are we?' interrupted the girl. Her name was Sarah Jane Smith. She was an independantly minded freelance journalist from the planet Earth in the twentieth century, and she had been the Doctor's more or less unwilling companion on a number of adventures.

She was already regretting that she had let the Doctor talk her into this trip. He had persuaded her with the promise of a fascinating visit to a picturesque and primitive planet, just making the transition from feudal savagery to technological civilisation.

Sarah looked round disgustedly. 'We're not in your precious Citadel of Peladon at all, we're in another rotten gloomy old tunnel!' For some reason tunnels seemed to feature largely in their adventures—and there was usually something nasty at the other end.

'I'm afraid the scanner must still be on the blink.'

'There's more than the scanner on the blink,' muttered Sarah darkly.

'I'm afraid the spatial co-ordinates must have slipped a bit,' said the Doctor apologetically. 'We may not actually be *in* the Citadel, but we're not far away. It's built on the peak of a mountain, you see, and the mountain is honeycombed with mining tunnels.'

'I don't suppose we could just get back in the TARDIS and go home?'

'Have a heart, Sarah, I've been looking forward to a return visit to Peladon for ages.'

The Doctor set off, and Sarah sighed and followed him.

Silently the watching guard slipped away.

In the main cavern a party of miners was setting up the sonic cannon, supervised by Eckersley and Vega Nexos.

Ettis looked on gloomily. Beside him was an older man, a burly, thick-set miner, with an air of natural authority. This was Gebek, leader of the Miners' Guild. Fiercely loyal both to his Queen and to the miners he led, he was having a difficult time reconciling the conflicting claims.

They looked up as Queen Thalira swept in, attended by Blor, her Champion, Chancellor Ortron and a squad of guards.

Gebek fell to one knee. 'We are honoured by your presence, Your Majesty.'

'And we are grateful for yours,' said Thalira regally. 'Can your miners be persuaded to overcome their fears?'

'The demonstration may help, Your Majesty. But as Ettis will tell you . . .'

Ettis threw himself on his knees before the Queen. 'I beg you not to permit this blasphemy, Your Majesty. I have *seen* the wrath of Aggedor . . .'

'You have seen the work of alien spies and saboteurs, agents of Galaxy Five,' interrupted Vega Nexos peevishly.

A guard ran in and threw himself down before Ortron. 'Aliens, my lord. They appeared in the tunnel as if by magic.'

Ortron turned to the Commander of the Queen's Guard. 'You heard him! There are aliens in the tunnels, enemies of Peladon and the Federation. They must be found and destroyed.'

As the guards ran from the cavern, Eckersley said, 'Everything is ready, Your Majesty. May we begin?'

Thalira inclined her head.

Eckersley said, 'If you will kindly keep your eyes on that section of wall over there . . . ' He pointed to the rock face on which the sonic cannon was trained.

Vega Nexos bent over the controls, there was a hum of power, and a circular chunk of the rock face exploded into fragments, instantly creating a miniature cave.

'Direct access to the main seam in a matter of moments,' said Eckersley proudly. 'Take weeks to do that by hand.'

A fierce light blazed from inside the newly created cave, and a shattering savage roar filled the cavern.

The Peladonians were transfixed with fear, but before anyone could stop him, Vega Nexos hurried forward to the gap. 'Do not be afraid, it is only some trickery . . . '

As he reached the hole there was another terrifying roar and a beam of brilliant light shot out. His body glowed brightly and vanished.

'You see,' screamed Ettis. 'It is the curse of Aggedor! Now do you believe?'

'Come, Your Majesty,' shouted Ortron. 'You must leave this place at once.' He led the Queen away, and the others hurried after them.

The Doctor stopped at a tunnel junction and looked thoughtfully around him.

'Go on, admit it, Doctor,' said Sarah. 'We're lost!'

'Well, a little mislaid possibly.'

'Why don't we go back to the TARDIS?'

'For two very good reasons, Sarah. Firstly I don't want to leave Peladon without seeing my old friend the King.'

'Name-dropper!'

'And secondly—we're lost!'

The Doctor led the grumbling Sarah along the tunnels. 'Cheer up, Sarah, we're nearly there.'

'As far as I'm concerned a tunnel is a tunnel is a tunnel,' muttered Sarah.

They heard voices and the sound of marching feet. 'That'll be the palace guard,' said the Doctor cheerfully. 'We'll be all right now.'

A squad of savage-looking soldiers, armed with spears, swords and pikes, swung round a bend in the tunnel.

'Don't run,' said the Doctor. 'As soon as I explain who I am . . .'

They heard the voice of the guard Captain. 'There they are! Kill them!'

'I've changed my mind,' shouted the Doctor. 'Run!'

The guards clattered after them as they fled down the tunnels. There were tunnel openings on all sides and the Doctor took first one and then another, apparently at random. His last choice seemed to be a bad one, since the tunnel ended in a blank wall, in which was set a single flaring torch.

They could hear the sound of the guards running up behind them. 'We're trapped, Doctor,' gasped Sarah.

'Oh no we're not,' said the Doctor cheerfully. 'I've been here before.' He reached up and twisted the torch-holder. It turned sideways, a section of wall slid back and they hurried through.

The door closed behind them and the pursuing guards turned the corner to find only a blank wall.

The Doctor and Sarah were in a dark and gloomy chamber, lit by flaring torches. The walls were decorated with rich tapestries, and at the far end was an altar, dominated by an immense stone statue, a bear-like beast with a single terrifying horn.

'There we are, Sarah,' said the Doctor. 'The Temple of Aggedor in the very heart of the Citadel of Peladon.'

'Very impressive. What about those guards? I thought you said they knew you here?'

'Oh, just a little misunderstanding, I imagine we startled them. Take a look at old Aggedor, there he is bless him!' The Doctor beamed affectionately at the terrifying statue.

Sarah came to join him. 'Doesn't look very loveable to me.'

'Well, this is a symbolic Aggedor, the real animal is

very different.' The Doctor stared up at the statue. 'You know, when I first came here, Peladon was just on the point of joining the Galactic Federation. There was a good deal of trouble . . . '

'Not now, Doctor,' whispered Sarah suddenly.

The Doctor was hurt, 'Well, of course, if you don't want to hear about it.'

'It isn't that, Doctor—but I think there's going to be some more trouble. Look!'

The Doctor turned.

Armed soldiers were filling the door to the temple.

As they were marched into the throne room the Doctor was saying cheerfully, 'Don't worry, Sarah, as soon as we see King Peladon . . . '

He broke off in astonishment, at the sight of the slender young woman on the throne.

The bearded figure beside the throne stepped forward. 'You stand accused of both sabotage and of sacrilege. Do you wish to confess, before you die?'

'No, we don't,' said Sarah spiritedly. 'I don't know what you're talking about.'

'Silence, slave. I addressed your master.'

'He's not my master,' said Sarah indignantly.

Ortron ignored her, glaring at the Doctor from beneath bushy eyebrows. 'Well, alien?'

The Doctor bowed low before the throne. 'May I ask who I have the honour of addressing?'

'I am Ortron, Chancellor and High Priest. This is Her Majesty Queen Thalira of Peladon.'

The Doctor bowed again. 'And *King* Peladon?'

'King Peladon was my father,' said Thalira. 'I was the child of his old age. He died when I was still a baby.'

'Name those who sent you alien,' boomed Ortron, 'and your life may yet be spared.'

The Doctor waved him away. 'Yes, yes, in a minute,

old chap.' He turned back to the Queen and said gently, 'I am called the Doctor, Your Majesty. Your father and I were good friends long before you were born.'

Thalira looked wonderingly at him. 'I have heard stories of the Doctor since I was a child. How you fought Grun and spared him, and tamed the sacred beast . . .'

'And so has every child on Peladon,' said Ortron scornfully.' What better disguise for an alien spy and saboteur than to claim to be a legendary hero of our people?'

The Doctor sighed. 'You really are a suspicious old fellow, aren't you?'

Ortron's face flushed with anger at the Doctor's insolence. Turning to the guard Captain he roared, 'Take these alien spies away and cut off their heads!'

2

Aggedor Strikes Again

Guards seized their arms, and began to drag them out.

Then a strange figure bustled into the throne room, and bowed before the throne.

Sarah gasped. 'Doctor, what's that?'

'The answer to all our troubles. Alpha Centauri!'

The Ambassador swung round, his tentacles waving wildly. 'Doctor! Is it really you?'

'Indeed it is!' Shaking off the astonished guards, the Doctor went over to his old friend. 'Alpha Centauri, my dear fellow! What a well-timed entrance!'

'It's like a miracle, Doctor! All these years, and you haven't changed a bit!'

'Neither have you. A touch of grey in the tentacles, perhaps, but still the same old Alpha.'

To Sarah's astonishment, the Doctor enfolded the many-tentacled alien in an affectionate hug, which was affectionately returned by all six tentacles.

'Ambassador!' boomed Ortron, reprovingly.

Alpha Centauri swung round. 'Forgive me, Chancellor, Your Majesty.'

'I take it these aliens are known to you, Ambassador?' asked Thalira.

'Not the, er—female?' Alpha Centauri blinked enquiringly at the Doctor, who nodded. 'Not the female, Your Majesty, she's of no importance. But this is most certainly the Doctor, a good friend of your father and of

Peladon.'

Thalira inclined her head. 'Very well. We shall release the aliens into your custody, Ambassador. But we shall expect a full explanation of their presence on Peladon.'

Alpha Centauri bowed and fluttered his tentacles. 'Of course, Your Majesty.' He turned to the Doctor. 'Come with me, please, Doctor. You may bring the female.'

Sarah stood her ground. 'Well, I don't think it's good enough. I think we're owed an apology, for the way we've been treated . . .'

'Not now, Sarah,' said the Doctor warningly. 'Come along.' Grabbing her by the hand, he pulled her after Alpha Centauri. As they left, Ortron approached the throne. 'It is not wise to trust this alien, Your Majesty. Even if he is the Doctor—was he not the one who helped persuade Peladon to join the Federation, and so caused all our troubles? Why has he come here again? Will he not bring still more trouble with him?'

Thalira said coldly, 'If the Doctor is our enemy, he will soon betray himself. We shall not learn of his plans by chopping off his head. See that he is watched.'

There was a secret passage from the mines into the Citadel. Gebek was in that passage now, together with Ettis and a squad of armed miners. Ettis was one of the leaders of a resistance movement, sworn to drive the aliens from Peladon. Gebek was sympathetic to their aims, but still hoped to reach the same results by peaceful means.

It was with that aim that he was about to enter the Citadel now. Ettis had no faith in his mission. 'Gebek, for the last time, will you listen? Even if you reach the Queen, it will do no good. She and Ortron are puppets of the Federation.'

'We must *try*,' said Gebek determinedly. 'If I can only talk to the Queen . . .'

'All right. But if your talking fails, Gebek—we fight.'

Gebek clamped a massive hand on his arm. 'There will be no fighting, not yet. You will all wait for me here. When I have spoken to the Queen, we shall talk again.'

Ettis waited till he was out of earshot. 'Gebek is a good man, but he is too trusting, too patient. We shall give him time to get clear. Then while he is talking, we shall *act*.'

From the low growl of assent, it was clear that the others were with him.

Gebek marched boldly along the corridors until he walked straight into a squad of palace guards. Outraged, they seized him. 'Take him to the Chancellor,' ordered the squad leader.

Gebek offered no resistance. It was what he wanted, after all.

Not far away, the Doctor and Sarah were heading for that part of the Citadel assigned to visiting aliens. Sarah was still protesting. 'I don't see why I should put up with being treated like this. And as for your friend there!' She nodded towards Alpha Centauri, who was leading the way down the corridor. ' "The female is of no importance," indeed!'

The Doctor grinned. 'I knew you wouldn't care for that! Still, you should be grateful to Alpha Centauri, Sarah, they go in for rough justice on Peladon. Chop off your head and apologise afterwards.'

Sarah refused to be consoled. 'If you hadn't missed the target by about five hundred yards and fifty years, we wouldn't be in all this trouble.'

In an anteroom just off the throne room, Gebek stood before Ortron under guard.

Ortron stared disdainfully at him. 'You know that the Citadel is forbidden to those of lowly rank?'

Gebek chuckled, 'Reserved for you nobles eh? And your *masters*, the Federation aliens, of course.'

Ortron flushed with anger. 'Do not be insolent, Gebek! Why did you come here?'

'I must speak with the Queen.'

'You should have petitioned for an audience in the proper way.'

'And endure endless delay? Things are too urgent for the proper way. I must see the Queen *now*—for the good of all Peladon.'

Such was Gebek's sincerity, that even Ortron was convinced. 'Very well.'

Ortron headed for the throne room, and Gebek followed him.

Ortron bowed before the throne. 'The miners' leader, Gebek, Your Majesty.'

Gebek fell to one knee. 'Forgive this intrusion, Your Majesty.'

Thalira said graciously. 'Why have you come here, Gebek?'

'To beg you to send the Federation aliens home. Otherwise there will be rebellion on Peladon.'

Gebek rose and began to plead his cause, not knowing that the rebellion had already begun.

The massive wooden doors to the armoury were permanently guarded. More than the weapons of the palace guard were kept there—the strange and deadly weapons of the Federation aliens were stored there too.

The guard before the doors marched up and down,

wondering sleepily how long it would be before he was relieved.

There was a patter of bare feet on stone, and half a dozen armed miners rushed along the corridor. Before the astonished sentry had time to react, they had pulled him down.

The communications room was in marked contrast to the rest of the Citadel. Instead of stone and torches and tapestries there was bright lighting and massed banks of control consoles. Modern living quarters were attached. Here the Federation representatives on Peladon were able to leave barbarism behind, and keep in touch with the affairs of the galaxy.

The Doctor had been introduced to Eckersley, and was now engaged in a heated discussion of the affairs of Peladon. 'It seems to me, the Federation has brought an awful lot of its troubles on itself.'

'That is less than fair, Doctor,' twittered Alpha Centauri.

Eckersley said, 'There have been so many difficulties.'

'All the same, it's over fifty years since Peladon joined the Federation and, from what you say yourself, all the miners have got to show for it, is more hard work for the same miserable rewards.'

'Peladon is a feudal society, Doctor. We attempt to bring them the benefits of our technology, but they are resistant to change.'

'And meanwhile we're under constant pressure from the Federation to step up the trisilicate production,' said Eckersley. 'It's essential to the war effort.'

The Doctor frowned. 'That's something else I don't like the sound of—this war with Galaxy Five. I thought the Federation was devoted to peace?'

'We were the victims of a vicious and unprovoked

attack,' said Alpha Centauri indignantly. 'We have tried to negotiate a peace treaty with Galaxy Five many times, but they refuse to listen.'

The Doctor sighed. Sometimes he felt he couldn't take his eyes off the universe for a moment without it getting into trouble. 'That's odd. This galaxy is much stronger than Five. They must know they'll lose in the end . . .'

Sarah went over to Eckersley. Something about his relaxed casualness appealed to her, and she couldn't see herself chatting with that octopus thing. 'What's so important about this trisilicate stuff, anyway?'

Eckersley looked at her in surprise. 'Most of Federation technology's based on it. Electronic circuitry, heat shields, inert micro-cell fibres, radionic crystallography . . . Whoever controls the supply of trisilicate will win this war—and the biggest deposits in the galaxy are right here on Peladon.'

'And you think someone wants to stop you mining it?'

'That's what Vega Nexos thought. He said it must be agents of Galaxy Five.'

The Doctor frowned. 'Well, I suppose it's possible, my dear chap, but—'

'Then where are they?' demanded Eckersley. 'And how are they managing to stay on Peladon undetected?'

There was the clangour of an alarm bell and an illuminated wall-map showed a flashing light. 'It's the armoury,' said Eckersley. He flicked on a monitor. 'Well, well, well.'

The monitor screen showed a group of miners. They were attacking the armoury door with pickaxes.

Soon the heavy wooden door was torn away—to reveal a solid sheet of gleaming metal.

'Alien work,' snarled Ettis. 'Preba, why don't you go and find an alien to open it.'

24

Preba grinned. He was the youngest of the group, and by far the most daring. Snatching up the sword of the unconscious guard, he hurried away.

Eckerlsey stood watching the scene on the monitor with amused indifference.

'You don't seem very worried,' said Sarah.

'Wasting their time, aren't they? Solid duralinium, that door. Triple-security electronic lock, remote-controlled from here.'

'King Peladon insisted that all the Federation weapons on the planet be stored there,' explained Alpha Centauri. 'So *we* insisted on providing proper protection.'

Eckersley said casually. 'Soon as old Ortron realises what's happening, he'll send a squad of guards to polish them off.'

Sarah was horrified. 'You're not just going to sit there and watch them get cut down?'

'Local politics, isn't it?' said Eckersley. 'Not my concern! In fact, we're strictly forbidden to interfere, eh, Alpha?'

The Doctor gave him a disgusted look, and headed for the door. 'I'll go, Sarah, you stay here.'

The Doctor opened the door—and Preba sprang through it, sword in hand.

Ignoring the Doctor, he advanced on Eckersley. 'Alien engineer—you will open the armoury door for us.'

'Not a chance,' said Eckersley calmly.

'Open the door or you will die!'

As Preba advanced, sword raised, the Doctor tripped him, twisted the sword from his hand and put him in an armlock.

'Thanks,' said Eckersley. 'Pretty handy for an old feller, aren't you?'

Alpha Centauri's tentacles were quivering in

agitation. 'You see the kind of dangers we face here, Doctor? Peladon is still a barbarous and primitive planet.'

'Maybe so, but its people have always been intensely loyal to the throne. If the miners have been driven to taking up arms, I should like to know why.' The Doctor looked at his captive. 'Well? Will you tell me?'

Preba tried unsuccessfully to break free, but said nothing.

'He's a fanatic,' said Eckersley contemptuously. 'He won't even talk to you.'

'Then perhaps he'd like to explain himself to the Queen,' said the Doctor grimly. 'Come on, you.' Tightening his grip, he marched Preba out of the door. 'You'd better stay here, Sarah. Alpha Centauri will look after you, won't you, old chap?'

'It will be my pleasure, Doctor.'

As the Doctor left, Alpha Centauri moved closer to Sarah.

Instinctively she shrunk away.

'I have been told that humans sometimes find the appearance of my species frightening,' said Alpha Centauri sadly. 'Yet I assure you, we are a peace-loving and amiable race.'

There was such pathos in the voice, that Sarah couldn't help smiling. 'I'm sorry. I didn't mean to be rude. This place is making me a bit jumpy.'

Alpha Centauri laid a reassuring tentacle on her arm. Strangely, Sarah discovered that she didn't mind at all.

In the throne room, Gebek was getting nowhere. Everything he said seemed to bounce straight off Ortron's opposition, without ever getting through to the Queen.

'I tell you this, Gebek,' said Ortron finally. 'Your rulers have decided to support the Federation. It is not for such as you to question their commands.'

'The people have had enough of the Federation and its commands,' said Gebek desperately. 'There will be armed rebellion!'

He looked appealingly at the throne, and Thalira said sadly, 'Will *you* rebel against me, Gebek?'

'I am loyal to the throne, Your Majesty, but . . .'

'Then order your miners to return to work,' snapped Ortron.

A panic-striken guard rushed into the throne room. 'Lord Ortron, armed miners have attacked the armoury. We drove them off and they escaped into the tunnels.'

'Not all of them,' said another voice. The Doctor marched Preba into the throne room.

Gebek stared at the prisoner in horror. 'Preba! What have you and those other fools done?' He turned to the Queen. 'Your Majesty, I swear I knew nothing of this.'

'We have the truth of it now, Gebek,' sneered Ortron. 'It is too late for your lies. You brought these men into the Citadel—then came here to distract our attention while they attacked.'

Gebek gave the Queen an anguished look. 'It is true that I came here with them, but I ordered them to wait in the tunnels.'

Ortron waved towards the Captain of the Guard. 'They are traitors. Take them away and execute them immediately.'

The Doctor kept a firm grasp of his prisoner. 'Now just a moment, Chancellor. I brought this man here to talk to the Queen, not to have his head cut off.'

'Silence, Doctor! We have heard enough from traitors. These men have invaded the Citadel and carried arms against Her Majesty. Our laws demand their execution. Take them away!'

As the guard came forward to take the Doctor's prisoner, the Doctor released Preba and shoved him towards the door. At the same time he grabbed the guard, spun him round and sent him reeling into

27

his fellows.

Seizing his opportunity, Gebek made a run for it. A guard raised his spear, Gebek's broad back a clear target before him.

The Doctor reached out and knocked his arm aside, and the spear went wide. By the time the guards had sorted themselves out and surrounded the Doctor, Gebek and Preba had disappeared. There was more than one secret passage in and out of the Citadel.

Ortron advanced menacingly on the Doctor. 'So, you are in league with traitors after all then, Doctor. Since you have helped them to escape, you shall die in their place.'

'You really are very ungrateful, Ortron,' said the Doctor reprovingly. 'I've just saved you from a serious political mistake.' He turned towards the throne. 'The miners are already on the point of rebellion. How would they react if Gebek, their beloved leader, was killed by the Queen's guards in the Queen's throne room?' The Doctor paused, to let the impact of his words sink in. 'He would have become a martyr, the inspiration for a people's revolution. And believe me, Your Majesty, there will be revolution and civil war on Peladon—unless you let me help you.'

'And how will you do that?'

'To begin with, by proving that the manifestations of Aggedor are caused by some kind of trickery. I'd like to examine the spot where he last appeared.'

Thalira considered. 'Very well, Doctor, we will trust you—for the moment. Blor, our Champion, will be your escort.'

Blor stalked over to the Doctor and took up a position behind him.

The Doctor looked up at the giant warrior a little apprehensively, wondering if Blor's function was that of escort or of guard. 'Splendid! Ready when you are, old chap.'

28

As they left the throne room, Ortron turned to the guard Captain. 'Send out patrols to all the mines and caves. I want Gebek—and anyone with him—captured or killed.'

In his enthusiasm, the Doctor had quite forgotten Sarah. Eckersley went off to find out what was going on, and returned with an account of events in the throne room. 'As far as I can gather, he's gone off to take a look in the quarry.'

'Leaving me to twiddle my thumbs,' said Sarah bitterly. 'Typical!'

'Well, at least he seems to have talked himself out of trouble,' said Eckersley.

'And into a lot more, I shouldn't wonder. Will he be all right?'

'As long as Aggedor doesn't get him. Well, I've got work to do.'

Eckersley drifted off, and Alpha Centauri said consolingly, 'I know you are worried about your friend the Doctor, but I assure you it will be safer for you to remain here.'

'Safer?'

'The Doctor has made an enemy of Chancellor Ortron —and that puts you in danger as well.'

'Ortron doesn't rule here. What about Queen Thalira?'

'Ortron holds the real power on Peladon,' explained Alpha Centauri. 'Thalira is young—and a female. I fear she is little more than a figurehead.'

'She's still the Queen. It's time she learned to stand up for herself.' Sarah sighed. 'Oh dear, I do hope the Doctor's all right.'

Ettis was hurrying through the cavern, laying a series of carefully placed charges, connecting them with a long trailing wire. Just as his task was finished he heard footsteps, and ducked into hiding behind a pillar of rock.

The Doctor and Blor appeared and Blor pointed mutely to the great hole blasted in the wall.

The Doctor nodded understandingly. 'I see, this is the place is it? Let's take a look inside.'

Blor hung back.

'Now, now,' said the Doctor. 'Don't tell me you're frightened, a big chap like you!' He led the way into the cave.

Behind his pillar, Ettis smiled. 'The alien and the Queen's Champion. They shall be sacrificed to Aggedor!'

The Doctor crawled into the cave, followed by Blor. Fishing a torch from his pockets, he looked around him. He picked up a piece of loose rubble and examined it. 'Practically pure trisilicate. No wonder the Federation are so keen. And you say this light that killed Vega Nexos came from in here?'

Blor nodded.

The Doctor shone his torch around the cave. 'Then there should be some trace of whatever's doing it . . .'

Gebek ran into the main cave to see Ettis connecting his wires to an old-fashioned plunger detonator. 'Ettis! What do you think you're doing?'

'I am restoring the mountain, to appease the spirit of Aggedor.' Before Gebek could stop him, Ettis thrust down the plunger and there was the rumble of an explosion.

Inside the cave, the sudden vibration knocked the Doctor off his feet. Picking up his torch, he shone it around and saw that the cave entrance had disappeared.

Blor lay half-stunned on the other side of the cave.

The Doctor went over to him. 'Are you all right?'

Blor grunted, and stumbled to his feet.

30

'We'd better start digging ourselves out,' said the Doctor. 'It looks like a long job, I'm afraid.'

They went to the spot where the entrance had once been and started clawing aside the rubble with their hands. The Doctor wondered if they would get clear before the air ran out.

Suddenly a bright light illuminated the darkness of the cave. The Doctor turned. Glaring out at them from the rock face was the terrifying form of Aggedor.

Blor fell to his knees in awe. A fierce ray of light shot out from the glowing image . . .

3

The Fugitives

The fierce glow faded as quickly as it had come, the snarling figure of Aggedor disappeared, and the cave returned to darkness. There was no sign of Blor's body.

The Doctor began heaving frantically at the rocks blocking the mouth of the cave. There was less chance than ever, now that he was alone—but he had to try . . .

Gebek looked despairingly at Ettis. 'Is there no end to your madness? First the armoury, now this!'

The eyes of Ettis held the mad glare of the fanatic. 'I have given the cave back to the mountain,' he boasted. 'I have made sacrifices to Aggedor!'

'Sacrifices?'

'Blor, the Queen's Champion, and one of the aliens. Both entered the cave, just before I set off the charge.'

Gebek grabbed him by the arm. 'Which alien, Ettis?'

'One of the new ones, a tall man with white hair.'

'The Doctor—our only friend! He saved my life. Come on, we've got to get him out.'

They ran to the blocked entrance and began pulling away the rocks.

Inside the cave, the Doctor was doing the same, working alone in stifling darkness.

Ettis stood up mopping his forehead. 'It's useless. There is nothing we can do.'

Gebek looked round for inspiration—and saw the abandoned sonic cannon on the other side of the cavern. 'We can reopen the cave with that!'

'You don't know how it works.'

'I saw the demonstration.'

'If you make a mistake, you'll kill your alien friend.'

Gebek went over to the cannon, studying the controls, trying to remember how Vega Nexos had operated them. Gebek took more interest in alien technology than most miners, realising that it was bound to come eventually. Uncertainly, his hands moved over the controls. He switched on the machine and it began to hum with power.

Inside the cave the fierce light appeared again, and the snarling form of Aggedor reappeared on the cave wall. There was a shattering roar—which blended with the crackling sound of a sonic explosion as a chunk of the cave door was blasted away.

Aggedor gave another fierce roar and the Doctor didn't hesitate. Diving straight forward, he went through the newly blasted hole like an acrobat going through a circus hoop. He hit the ground with his shoulder, rolled over and tumbled down the rock slide. Gebek helped him to his feet and hurried him away.

In the communications room, Alpha Centauri was doing his best to entertain Sarah. They were standing before an illuminated wall-map of the Citadel and the area all around it. 'This map here shows the new refinery. It is fully automated, a most magnificent installation. Unfortunately, we have not yet produced enough trisilicate to make use of it, but as soon as we do . . .'

Sarah wasn't really listening. 'The Doctor's been gone an awfully long time.'

'Of course, I myself am no engineer,' Alpha Centauri continued. 'Only Eckersley fully understands the new equipment. He will be happy to explain everything.'

'I'll look forward to it,' said Sarah absently.

Suddenly an electronic voice came from a speaker.

In calm and placid computer tones it announced, 'Emergency! Emergency! This is the automatic scanning system. I have just detected a rockfall in the main cavern, produced by the unauthorised use of explosives. Emergency!'

Sarah ran to the map. 'That's where the Doctor's gone. I knew it—something's happened. I'm going to find him.'

'It really is unwise,' twittered Alpha Centauri. 'I am sure the authorities will mount a proper rescue operation.'

Sarah said, 'On this planet? I don't trust any of them.' She looked again at the map. 'Now, we're here and the Doctor's here—so if I take these tunnels . . .'

She ran from the room.

Alpha Centauri's tentacles rippled in distress. 'These Earth females seem to have a distressing tendency to rash action.' He went over to the console and touched a control. 'Engineer Eckersley!' he said plaintively. '*Please* return to the control room immediately.'

The Doctor looked thoughtfully at the sonic cannon. 'So you got me out with this, eh? Very enterprising of you.'

'I owed you my life,' said Gebek gruffly. 'Now we are even.'

Ettis tried to pull Gebek away. 'All right, you've paid your debt. Now let's go before Ortron's guards find us.'

'Wait! I can give you still more help—if you'll let me.'

'Why should you wish to help us?'

'For the good of Peladon,' said the Doctor simply.

'What could you do?'

'Find out who's using Aggedor to frighten your miners.'

'No one *uses* Aggedor,' hissed Ettis. 'His spirit is angry with us.'

Ignoring him, the Doctor turned to Gebek. 'If you can get your men back to work, I think I can persuade the Federation to improve conditions now, not wait till the war is over.'

Gebek said, 'Perhaps. But the miners will not work while Aggedor is angry.'

'Exactly—and that's just what someone wants. Do you think it's just coincidence that Aggedor appeared in that cave the moment I started to investigate?'

Suddenly Ettis shouted, 'Look out—soldiers!'

A patrol of guards had entered the cavern through one of the side tunnels. 'That's Gebek!' shouted one of the guards. 'There he is—kill him!'

The guards rushed forward to the attack. Fanatical as ever, Ettis rushed to meet them, striking down their leader with his pickaxe.

Gebek clubbed down another with a massive fist, and the Doctor grabbed the third and hurled him into his fellows. Most of the squad went down in a tangle of arms and legs.

'Quick, this way!' yelled Gebek. The Doctor and the two miners ran from the cavern.

Sarah had been overconfident about finding her way from communications room to cavern. One tunnel looks very like another: she took a number of wrong turnings and soon she was completely lost.

She turned a corner, went through a stone arch and found herself facing a massive metal door set into a wall of rock. There was a thick, plasti-glass panel set into the top half of the door. A light shone behind the panel, and Sarah thought she could see someone moving.

She hammered on the door with her fists. 'Hello, there! I'm lost. Can you help me?'

There was no reply. Sarah stared through the panel, and caught a glimpse of a massive, distorted shape moving hurriedly away. Whatever it was it certainly didn't look human . . .

The light behind the door went out.

Sarah hammered again. 'I know you're in there! Look, I only want to find my way out of these tunnels.'

Suddenly a spider's web of pulsing light beams sprang up, trapping Sarah in a cage of light. High-pitched discordant noises attacked her ears, lights whirled and flashed before her eyes, in a combined assault that seemed to overwhelm her senses.

Eyes tightly closed, hands clamped over her ears, Sarah sank slowly to the ground.

Eckersley strolled into the communications room. 'All right, all right, here I am, Alpha, old son. What's all the panic?'

Alpha Centauri's tentacles were positively flailing in agitation. 'There has been an explosion in the cavern, where the Doctor was. Sarah went to find him, and neither has returned.'

Eckersley went over to the control console, where a light was flashing. 'There's an alarm signal coming from the refinery. Probably those miners again.'

He switched on a monitor. Sarah's huddled figure appeared on the screen, her distorted face illuminated by flashing lights. 'Good grief, what's she doing there? She must have triggered off the defence system.' Eckersley's hands flicked switches, the lights and noises stopped, and Sarah's face relaxed into unconsciousness.

'What a catastrophe!' twittered Alpha Centauri. 'Has she been harmed?'

'Depends how long she was under it—if it was too long her brains could be scrambled. We'd better go and get her.'

In a disused mine shaft the Doctor was sitting in as an honorary member of a sort of miners' council. Torchlight flickered on grimy work-worn faces. Gebek and the rest were telling him of their troubles. 'Our lives have always been the same, Doctor. Work and sleep, little more. We earn barely enough to feed our families.'

'The Federation promised us things would improve,' said young Preba.

'So they did—for the nobles. We got nothing, as usual!'

There was an angry rumble of assent from the other miners.

Ettis seized his chance. 'And now they bring their alien machines to rip the heart from Aggedor's sacred mountain. No wonder he is angry with his people.'

The Doctor shook his head. 'I don't believe that. I think the Aggedor you've seen is a piece of technological trickery.'

'Then who is causing it?' demanded Gebek.

'I don't know, but I'm determined to find out.'

'And what do we do meanwhile?'

'Nothing. Sit tight and wait—and no more idiotic tricks like that attack on the armoury.'

He looked accusingly at Ettis, who said defensively, 'We nearly succeeded!'

'You never stood a chance. The armoury doors are electronically operated from the communications room.

That sort of thing just gets people killed for nothing. Just give me a chance to sort things out peacefully.'

Gebek said firmly, 'We will take your advice, Doctor. There will be no more fighting, is that understood? Ettis?'

Ettis gave a surly nod of assent.

The Doctor stood up. 'Splendid! Now, I want a chance to have a talk with the Queen—without Ortron breathing down my neck.'

'There are many secret ways to the Citadel. Preba knows them all. He will guide you. Preba, come. The rest of you stay here and wait for news. Come, Doctor.'

Gebek, Preba and the Doctor moved away. When they were safely out of earshot, Ettis summoned a group of his most fanatical followers around him. 'I say we attack again. This time we shall succeed. We know how to open the armoury door now—thanks to the Doctor.'

Alpha Centauri and Eckersley helped Sarah to her feet. She stared dazedly at them.

'Are you all right, love?' asked Eckersley.

'I think so. What happened to me?'

'You set off the automatic defence system. Just a bit of magic to scare off intruding natives.'

'All that just to protect your machinery. You're very keen on security, aren't you?'

'Have to be, love, on a planet like this. What were you doing here anyway?'

'I was lost, I saw somebody in there and I wanted to ask the way.'

Eckersley shook his head. 'Nobody in there, the place is on shutdown.'

'I tell you I saw a light, and someone moving!'

'Hallucinations. After what you've just been through . . .'

'I tell you I did see someone—before that thing went off.'

Alpha Centauri interrupted. 'If you are well enough to move, I suggest we return to the control room.'

Sarah took a few steps and found that although still giddy she could walk perfectly well. Suddenly she remembered her original quest. 'What about the Doctor. Have you heard what happened?'

'No. Let's return to the communications room. By now there may be news of him.'

The Doctor and the two miners were moving swiftly and silently along the tunnels. Gebek stopped at a point where several tunnels joined and raised his hand. 'Listen!'

They heard the tramp of marching feet. 'Soldiers,' whispered Gebek. 'They are searching the tunnels for us.'

The Doctor sighed. 'Old Ortron never gives up, does he? Can we lose them?'

'They are blocking the route we need to follow.'

Preba said, 'Don't worry, I'll lead them away from you.'

'No Preba. If they catch you, you'll be killed.'

Preba grinned cheekily. 'A squad of clodhopping guards catch me? I've played in these tunnels since I was a boy.'

Before Gebek could stop him he ran forward to a point where the soldiers could see him.

A yell went up.

'There he is!'

'After him!'

The soldiers broke into a run, and Preba sped fleet-footed in front of them, leading them down a side tunnel.

Gebek waited until they were out of sight. 'Wait here, Doctor—I'll check if it's safe. There may be more patrols.'

And indeed there were. Gebek turned into another tunnel, and ran straight into two more guards.

They closed in on him immediately. One of them held a sword to his ribs. 'You're under arrest, Gebek. Come with us.'

The soldiers led him past the tunnel where the Doctor was hiding. As they passed, the Doctor reached out, putting a hand on each man's shoulder, long fingers probing for a nerve-centre. The soldiers stiffened and slumped unconscious to the floor.

Gebek stared at the Doctor in astonishment.

'Venusian karate,' said the Doctor apologetically. 'Comes in useful sometimes. Lead the way Gebek, I want to see the Queen!'

In the throne room, Queen Thalira was undergoing yet another harangue from her Chancellor. 'Blor is dead, Your Majesty, slain, like the others, by the wrath of Aggedor. And all this trouble began when the Doctor arrived on Peladon.'

'Perhaps the spirit of Aggedor *is* angry. But that does *not* prove that the Doctor is our enemy, Ortron.'

'He was seen with Gebek and the rebels. He has escaped to join them.'

Thalira said wearily, 'Why Ortron? Why would he turn against us. He was my father's friend. He said he came to help us.'

'A trick to gain your confidence. After so long a time, who can be sure it is the same man?'

Thalira sank back on her throne. 'What is your counsel, Lord Ortron?' she asked wearily.

Ortron said impressively. 'The revolt must be crushed, and crushed now. The Doctor must be found— and executed!'

4

The Hostage

Sarah was still grumbling as they came along the corridor to the communications room. 'All right, so you need some kind of alarm system at the refinery. Does it have to be something that drives people out of their minds?'

'You've got to remember we're strangers on this planet,' said Eckersley patiently. 'And we're not too popular. We've got to protect ourselves.'

'Most of the Peladonians are still close to barbarism,' said Alpha Centauri. 'They have a great distrust of progress.'

Sarah stopped and turned to face him. 'Maybe that's because they're not getting anything out of it. You've got to convince them progress will give them a better life.'

'It's no good, Sarah,' said Eckersley. 'Force is all they understand.'

As if to give emphasis to his words, Ettis sprang around out from his hiding place behind an arras, and struck Eckersley down with the hilt of his sword.

Eckersley groaned and fell, and Ettis menaced Alpha Centauri with his sword blade.

'Help, help, we are being attacked,' shrieked the Ambassador.

'Silence, alien. Into the communications room, both of you.' Leaving Eckersley where he had fallen, Ettis herded Alpha Centauri and Sarah through the doorway.

Once they were inside, Ettis said threateningly, 'Do as you are told and you won't be harmed. I want you to open the Federation armoury door.'

'That is out of the question,' said Alpha Centauri primly. 'Natives of primitive planets are forbidden access to sophisticated weapons.'

Ettis held his sword to Sarah's throat. 'Open that door!'

'Only Eckersley knows how to operate the controls, and you have rendered him unconscious. I cannot do as you ask.'

'I advise you to try—if you wish to save the life of your fellow alien.' Again the sword menaced Sarah.

Reluctantly Alpha Centauri moved to the control panel.

The sentry outside the armoury was no more wary than his predecessor—he wasn't expecting a second attack, so soon after the first. The sudden rush of attacking miners took him completely by surprise and, like the sentry before him, he was soon overwhelmed.

The attackers set to work on the wooden outer door, which had been hurriedly repaired after the first attack.

Ettis brought his sword closer to Sarah. 'Hurry, alien —or must I prove that I mean what I say?'

Alpha Centauri knew perfectly well how to open the armoury door; as Ettis suspected, he had been playing for time. Reluctantly he reached out a tentacle for the door control and pressed it—and at the same time another tentacle triggered the alarm.

The wooden door had been wrenched open by now. The miners were waiting impatiently. Suddenly there was a click and the gleaming metal door slid back.

Triumphantly the attackers poured into the armoury, a small metal chamber whose walls were lined with racks of hand-blasters. At the same time the clangour of an alarm bell ran out. Hurriedly the miners snatched blasters from the racks and passed them out to their waiting fellows.

A guard Captain rushed into the throne room. 'Lord Ortron, Your Majesty! There has been a second attack on the armoury. The rebels have opened the inner door.'

Ortron turned to Thalira. 'You see, Your Majesty? This is what comes of softness with the common people. The rebellion has begun!'

And indeed, the first shots of the rebellion had already been fired. Summoned by the alarm, a squad of palace guards ran towards the armoury—only to be shot down by rebels, armed with Federation blasters. Several of the guards fell, and the rest turned and fled.

The triumphant rebels headed back to the mines.

Ettis stood at the door to the communications room, listening to the distant rattle of blaster fire and the shouts of the guards. He rounded angrily on Alpha Centauri. 'You have betrayed me—you set off the alarm.'

Alpha Centauri backed away. 'I warned you I did not fully understand the controls. It was an accident . . .'

Ettis raised his sword, Alpha Centauri cowered back, and Sarah stepped between them. 'What does it matter now? You've got what you came for. Why don't you

43

escape while you've still got the chance?'

'Excellent advice, alien,' snarled Ettis. 'I shall take you with me, as a hostage.'

Grabbing Sarah by the wrist, he dragged her from the room, along the corridor and around the corner out of sight.

Alpha Centauri followed cautiously. He stopped by the prone body of Eckersley. 'Engineer Eckersley, please. You must wake up!'

Eckersley moaned and stirred.

As the rebels pulled down the torch-holder to open the secret passage, Ettis ran along the corridor, dragging Sarah behind him.

'All is well? We have the weapons? Come then!'

Carrying the stolen blasters, the rebels hurried through the secret entrance.

Ettis watched them impatiently. Suddenly more guards appeared, running down the corridor towards them.

'Hurry!' yelled Ettis, and Sarah wrenched herself free and ran back down the corridor. Ettis set off in pursuit, realised he would only be captured himself, and darted back into the secret passage, closing the door behind him.

As he reached them, Ortron appeared. 'Seize her,' he called. 'Do not let her escape!'

'I don't want to escape,' protested Sarah. 'I've escaped already—from them!'

'Take her to the temple,' ordered Ortron. Guards grabbed hold of Sarah and dragged her away.

The Doctor and Gebek had just entered the secret tunnel when they met Ettis and his rebels, running the other way. Arms filled with blasters, they dashed past them down the tunnel. Gebek grabbed hold of Ettis, as he brought up the rear. 'Ettis what new madness is this?'

'It is victory, Gebek!' Triumphantly Ettis brandished a stolen blaster. 'Now we have Federation weapons, we shall see who rules on Peladon!' Pulling himself free, he hurried after the others.

Gebek looked after him despairingly. 'I must go with them, Doctor—perhaps I can prevent more bloodshed.'

'Yes, of course. It's all right, Gebek, I know where I am now.'

Gebek hurried off, and the Doctor went on down the tunnel. He would make for the passage that led to the temple, he decided.

Eckersley stood rubbing his aching head, looking despairingly around the looted armoury. 'That's really done it. With modern weapons in their hands, there's no end to the damage these lunatics can do.'

Alpha Centauri's tentacles drooped disconsolately. 'It is all my fault. I shall resign immediately.'

'Well, it's done now. No use going on about it.'

'I could have faced death for myself, Eckersley, in an honourable cause. But he threatened the Doctor's friend, and I was unable to stand by and see violence inflicted on a fellow creature.'

Eckersley rubbed his still-aching head. 'Where is the girl, anyway?'

'Ettis took her as a hostage. Presumably she is still his prisoner.'

The guard Captain said importantly, 'No, Excellency, she was captured by the guards. Chancellor Ortron believes that she was helping the rebels.'

'Where is she now?'

The guard Captain lowered his voice in awe. 'She has been taken to the temple—for judgement.'

Sarah stood before the altar flanked by guards. Torch-light flickered on the snarling features of the great stone image of Aggedor.

From behind the altar, Ortron thundered. 'Admit it, you were in collusion with the rebel Ettis.'

'Of course I wasn't!'

'Was it not because of you that the Ambassador was forced to open the door to the armoury?'

'Well, I suppose it was, in a way, but . . .'

'So you admit your guilt!' thundered Ortron.

'The Ambassador *had* to open the door to save my life—Ettis said he'd kill me if he didn't do it. You can't say that means I was helping him.'

'You came to this planet to stir up the common people, to overthrow their rightful rulers, the nobility of Peladon. You joined forces with the traitor Ettis, while the Doctor allied himself with the other traitor, Gebek.'

Suddenly the Doctor stepped forward from the shadows. 'Forgive me, old chap, but you really have got things all wrong.'

Sarah said delightedly, 'Doctor, you're all right! They said you'd been blown up in the cavern.'

'I very nearly was, Sarah. Luckily Gebek got me out.'

'Ettis has just robbed the armoury . . .'

'I know. Gebek and I met him in the tunnels.'

Ortron was quick to seize on this damaging admission.

'So you admit your guilt, do you, Doctor?'

'My dear chap, you're really not listening,' said the Doctor soothingly. 'No one is admitting anything because there's nothing to admit. All the same, if you want my advise, you'll get on good terms with Gebek. Without him you'll have a full-scale rebellion on your hands in no time.'

'I need no advice from saboteurs,' growled Ortron.

'Your trouble is, you won't take advice from anyone! Just take us to the Queen, there's a good chap. We'll sort things out with Her Majesty.'

Ortron smiled. 'There is no need to trouble the Queen, Doctor. I shall deal with you myself!'

He cast incense onto the lamps that burned on the altar and their flames leaped high.

High Priest now, rather than Chancellor, Ortron bowed to the great statue of Aggedor. 'Oh mighty Aggedor, make known thy will! How shall we punish those who have offended against thee?'

The flames from the altar lamps illuminated the savage face of Aggedor with a lurid glow, so that the features seemed to writhe and snarl.

'Well, what did he say?' asked the Doctor interestedly.

'You have blasphemed against Aggedor, and by Aggedor shall you both be punished.'

'Both? That's a bit much, Sarah hasn't done anything.'

'She shares your guilt, and she shall share your punishment. Prepare the pit!'

Ortron stepped back, and temple guards came to heave upon the altar. They pushed it slowly aside revealing the mouth of the black pit beneath.

Alpha Centauri had been unable to gain entrance to the temple to help Sarah. Now he was in the throne room, pleading her cause to the Queen. 'Believe me, Your Majesty,' he concluded, 'Chancellor Ortron has totally misinterpreted the facts.'

Thalira considered. 'Engineer Eckersley, do you confirm the Ambassador's story?'

Eckersley fingered the bump at the back of his head. 'I'm afraid I can't confirm anything, Your Majesty. I got thumped on the head, and by the time I came round, it was all over.'

Alpha Centauri turned to him in surprise. 'But you do know that Sarah is not in league with the rebels.'

47

As usual, Eckersley was reluctant to stick his neck out. 'Seems pretty unlikely. Still, we know very little about her. You *were* forced to open the door because of the girl—it could all have been a put-up job.'

'The whole idea is absurd,' said Alpha Centauri vehemently. 'I assure Your Majesty that the girl was Ettis's prisoner, his hostage, not his accomplice.'

'I am prepared to trust your judgement, Ambassador,' said Thalira slowly. 'But what I believe is of little importance. Ortron is High Priest as well as Chancellor. In the precincts of the temple his power is absolute. There is nothing I can do.'

'But your Majesty,' protested Alpha Centauri, 'whatever your traditions, can you not overrule them in the name of mercy and justice? After all you are the Queen!'

'A Queen who is treated as a child,' said Thalira angrily.

Alpha Centauri bowed. 'Many things are changing on Peladon, Your Majesty. Perhaps this too is a thing that should change?'

Thalira rose to her feet. 'We shall go to the temple.'

The entrance to the pit was fully revealed by now. It gaped, dark and sinister, in the spot where the altar had stood.

'Cast them in!' ordered Ortron.

Guards seized the Doctor and Sarah, rushed them forwards, and thrust them over the edge of the pit. Arms and legs flailing, they fell down into darkness.

As the royal party approached the temple doors, guards stepped forward, barring their way with crossed pikes.

Thalira's eyes flashed with anger. 'I am the Queen! No doors are barred to me. Stand aside!' She strode determinedly forward and the astonished guards fell back.

Thalira marched determinedly into the temple. 'Chancellor Ortron, where is the alien girl? We demand that you release her!'

'You are too late, Your Majesty. The Doctor and the girl have gone to face the judgement of Aggedor!'

Ortron stepped aside and pointed to the sinister darkness of the pit.

Fortunately for the Doctor and Sarah, the pit was not so deep as it looked, and after a relatively short fall, they thudded onto a stone floor strewn thickly with straw.

The Doctor picked himself up. 'Sarah, are you all right?'

There was a groan from just beside him. 'Well, I'm bruised, but I don't think anything's broken.'

There was an arched doorway in the bottom of the pit, leading to what looked like a large dungeon.

'What are they going to do with us?' asked Sarah. 'Just leave us here?'

'I think there's a little more to it than that.'

'And what's that smell? Sort of musky—like the lion house at the zoo . . . '

Sarah broke off, realising what she was saying.

There was a low, coughing roar, and something stirred in the darkness of the dungeon.

'There's something down here with us, Doctor,' whispered Sarah. 'Something very large—and it's alive.'

'I know,' said the Doctor quietly. 'Don't move!'

He took a torch from his pocket and shone the beam around the dungeon.

As the light reached the far corner, there was an angry snarl. Rearing up in the darkness was the terrifying form of Aggedor—not a stone statue, or a ghostly manifestation, but the living beast.

Aggedor roared again and shambled towards them.

5

The Wrath of Aggedor

Eyes blazing with anger, Thalira confronted Ortron. 'Remove the Doctor and his friend from the pit at once, Ortron. We command it.'

A savage roar echoed out of the darkness. Ortron smiled and stroked his beard. 'Too late, Your Majesty. By now they have already paid the penalty for their crimes.'

Sarah shrank back against the side of the pit, while the Doctor spoke soothingly to Aggedor, in the hope of calming the great beast. They had met once before, when Aggedor had been used by the High Priest Hepesh in an attempt to prevent Peladon joining the Federation. It was incredible that the great beast had survived so long. It was even bigger now, its movements a little stiff, the fierce muzzle streaked with grey, but it was still a mighty and terrifying monster, capable of killing him with one blow of the razor-clawed paw.

That paw whizzed over the Doctor's head now. The Doctor ducked and leaped aside. 'Come along now, Aggedor, old chap. This isn't a very nice way to greet an old friend. You remember me, surely?'

Aggedor snarled and the paw slashed out again. 'I don't think he does, Doctor,' said Sarah nervously.

'You'd never believe it,' gasped the Doctor, 'but he

and I used to be the greatest of friends.'

Aggedor charged and the Doctor leaped aside. 'Of course—I remember now!'

Backing away, the Doctor took an old-fashioned gold watch from his pocket. At the same time, he began a low, crooning chant, strange-sounding words set to a haunting melody.

> 'Klokeda, partha, mennin klatch
> Ablark, araan, aroon
> Klokeeda shunna teerenatch
> Aroon, araan, aroon, araan
> Aroon, araan, aroon
> Aroon, araan, aroon, araan
> Aroon, araan, aroon.'

As he chanted, the Doctor spun the watch around on its chain, swinging it to and fro before Aggedor's eyes.

Gradually, the growls became fewer and changed to a low rumble, very much like a giant purr.

The Doctor beamed. 'That's better, old chap, remember me now, don't you?' He reached up and scratched Aggedor behind the ear.

Sarah let out a sigh of incredulous relief. 'You ought to be a lion-tamer, Doctor. How did you manage to do that?'

'Empathy—that and a bit of light hypnosis. Works wonders! Brings out his sweeter side—doesn't it, old chap?'

'What was that you were chanting? What did it mean?'

'It's an old Venusian lullaby,' said the Doctor solemnly. 'It means "Close your pretty eyes, my darling—well, three of them at least." Aggedor's very fond of it. Here, come and tickle his ears, Sarah.'

'No thanks. Look, this reunion is very touching, but what happens now?'

'Well, we were chucked down here to be judged by Aggedor—and I'd say the verdict was very much in our favour.' Standing below the pit shaft, the Doctor raised his voice. 'Hey, you up there! How about getting us out of here?'

After a moment the astonished face of a temple guard appeared over the edge of the pit. He was holding a lamp; its rays showed him the astonishing sight of the Doctor and Sarah, both alive and unharmed, with Aggedor standing peacefully between them. Almost dropping the lamp in his surprise, the guard hurried to Queen Thalira to report a miracle.

Some considerable time later, Alpha Centauri bustled into the communications room, 'Now that the Doctor is in good standing again, he will soon help us to clear up our problems.'

Eckersley looked up from the console. 'I admire your confidence. There's a gang of fanatics running round those tunnels, armed with our blasters. What's the Doctor going to do about that?' He paused. 'Anyway, political problems on Peladon aren't the Doctor's responsibility—they're yours.'

'That is true—and the situation is indeed deplorable. But what can I do? I am only an observer here, I have no powers.'

'I know what I'd do . . .' Eckersley turned back to his console. 'Still, I don't suppose you want me interfering.'

'Please, Eckersley, advise me. You are a man of decision. What would you do?'

'I'd get myself a bit of muscle. Get the Federation to send in security troops—a peace-keeping force. With them on the planet, you and the Doctor could make both sides see reason in no time.' Eckersley paused. 'Suit yourself, of course, I'm only an engineer. But I can tell you this. If things do go bad on this planet, then the Federation could lose its supply of trisilicate. And if that happens, they'll want to know why they weren't told

52

how serious the situation was getting in time for them to do something about it!'

'There is much good sense in what you say, Eckersley.'

'You've had a long and distinguished career on this planet. You were here at the very beginning, when they first joined the Federation. Be a pity to see it all end in an ugly political mess.' Eckersley stood up. 'You think it over. I must be off.'

'Where are you going?'

'I've just remembered something—the sonic cannon is still in the cavern, and it would make a pretty nasty piece of artillery in the wrong hands. I'm going to borrow a few guards and bring it back before the rebels get their hands on it.'

Eckersley went off and Alpha Centauri took his place at the console. The more he thought about Eckersley's advice, the more sensible it seemed. It would remove the crushing weight of responsibility from him—surely no one could blame him, as long as he reported the crisis in good time? He considered asking the Doctor's opinion—and then remembered something else Eckersley had said. Affairs on Peladon were not the Doctor's responsibility—they were the Ambassador's. He was an important Federation official, and it was time he started acting like one.

Tentacles quivering with decision, Alpha Centauri reached for the controls. 'This is the Federation Ambassador to the planet Peladon. Get me the emergency security channel—utmost priority!'

In the throne room, the Doctor and Sarah were spectators at a rare occasion. Chancellor Ortron was being given a royal telling-off. 'The Doctor and his companion have been most barbarously treated. Your conduct was unforgivable, Lord Ortron!

Ortron was outraged. 'But Your Majesty . . .'

'Silence, Chancellor. You chose to appeal to the judgement of Aggedor, and now you shall accept it. The Doctor is to be considered completely vindicated, and freed with your apologies.'

Ortron bowed stiffly, almost too angry to speak. 'As Your Majesty commands.' He bowed stiffly. 'Doctor, my apologies. Have I Your Majesty's permission to return to the temple?'

Thalira nodded dismissively, and Ortron turned and stalked from the throne room.

'Chairs and refreshments for our guests,' commanded Thalira.

Guards came forward with ornately carved chairs and a small table, setting them before the throne. Thalira waved her hand.

'Please be seated.'

The Doctor and Sarah sat, and a lady-in-waiting hurried forward with silver goblets and a flagon of wine. She poured wine for them both, and Thalira said, 'Please accept our apologies too, Doctor.'

The Doctor sipped his wine appreciatively. 'No apology is needed, Your Majesty. It was a great pleasure to meet Aggedor again.'

'What did you discover in your investigation at the mines? Did you learn who was behind the manifestations of Aggedor's spirit?'

'No, Your Majesty. But I did learn that the miners are so terrified that they are on the point of armed revolt. Gebek is your only hope now. Civil war is the last thing he wants.'

Sarah joined in. 'Gebek may want peace—but what about Ettis?'

'He's our main problem. He scored a success with that second raid on the armoury. He has weapons now, and all the young hotheads will be keen to follow him.'

Thalira seemed crushed by the responsibilities of

royalty. 'What do you advise, Doctor?'

'Send for Gebek and promise a better way of life for the miners. That will cut the ground from under Ettis's feet.'

'But Ortron says it is wrong to give in to the miners . . .'

'Ortron just wants to make sure that the benefits of joining the Federation go to him and his friends,' said Sarah. 'You've got to convince your people that the Federation means a better way of life for everyone.'

Thalira came to a decision. 'Can you get a message to Gebek for me?'

'I'll manage somehow, Your Majesty.'

'Tell him to come to the Citadel and meet with me in secret. I will hear the grievances of his people and do my best to remedy them.'

The Doctor rose. 'Thank you, Your Majesty. I'll just have a quick word with the Ambassador, and then I'll be on my way.' As Sarah rose to follow him the Doctor said, 'Why don't you stay and talk to the Queen, Sarah? Tell her about Women's Lib!'

Thalira looked at Sarah in puzzlement. 'What is this Women's Lib?'

Sarah smiled. 'It means Womens Liberation, Your Majesty. Women have been pushed around on Earth for a very long time, but it's all changing now.'

'Not on Peladon, it isn't,' said Thalira sadly. 'Traditionally the ruler is always a man. I was crowned only by default, since my father had no sons. Ortron holds the real power.'

'Only if you let him. You've got to stand up for yourself.'

'It would be different if I were a man—but since I am only a female . . .'

'There is nothing "only" about being female,' said Sarah indignantly. 'Never mind why they made you Queen—you are the Queen. Now you've got to learn to

55

act like one. I think you've made a pretty good start.'

In the mines far beneath the Citadel, Gebek was trying to control an unruly meeting without much success. It was Ettis the miners wanted to hear now.

Flushed with success, Ettis waved a stolen blaster. 'I say we attack now, capture the Citadel, force the Queen to listen to our demands—and expel the aliens from the planet.'

There was a roar of assent.

Gebek leaped to his feet. 'Do you think you can fight the entire Federation with a handful of stolen weapons?'

'And what is your advice?' sneered Ettis. 'More waiting?'

'Refuse to work! The Federation must have the trisilicate, that is our real strength. They'll put pressure on Ortron, force him to grant our demands.'

'Nonsense! They'll simply bring in technicians to mine the ore with their alien machines . . .' Suddenly Ettis broke off. 'Of course—the alien machine. We have a weapon that will force them to surrender to our demands.' He looked round the group. 'You and you, and you, come with me. You as well . . .'

Gebek looked on in alarm, as Ettis began selecting a squad of his most fanatical followers.

'You've sent for Federation troops?' The Doctor stared at Alpha Cenauri in disgust. 'What on Peladon poss-essed you to do a thing like that?'

'It seemed the only possible course of action at the time. Eckersley agreed . . .'

'He should have had more sense. Federation troops on the planet can only make things worse. I just hope we can get things sorted out before they arrive.'

Sarah came rushing in and said, 'Doctor , there was

something I meant to tell you. I got lost in the tunnels when I was looking for you and stumbled on to the refinery. I saw a light on and someone moving in there. Whoever is faking those Aggedor manifestations would need some very sophisticated equipment, right?'

'I should imagine so—and a very considerable power source as well.'

'Well, all of that could be hidden in the refinery.'

'But the refinery is closed down,' protested Alpha Centauri peevishly. 'It is empty.'

'Empty as far as you know,' said Sarah. 'Suppose somebody's in there? It would make a perfect hide-out.'

The Doctor rubbed his chin. 'It's an interesting theory, Sarah, and worth investigating. I'll try to check up on it later. Right now, I've got to find Gebek.'

A voice spoke from the doorway. 'So you plan to contact the rebels, Doctor?'

It was Ortron, with guards at his back. 'You may have deceived the Queen, Doctor. She is young and inexperienced. But you do not deceive me! You will remain in this Citadel.'

'Will you kindly get out of my way?' said the Doctor impatiently. A guard barred his way.

'You have the freedom of the Citadel, Doctor,' said Ortron, 'but that is all. Do not attempt to leave it. Be thankful you are not confined to one of its dungeons.'

Ortron turned and marched away and the guards followed him.

'Pompous old fool,' said Sarah disrespectfully. 'Are you going to do as he says?'

'No, of course not. It's vital I see Gebek before it's too late. Ortron's exceeding his authority anyway. Don't worry, Sarah, he won't dare to harm me now the Queen's on our side.'

Popping his head into the corridor the Doctor saw that Ortron and the guards were out of sight. 'Right, I'll be off, then.'

'Good luck, Doctor—and be careful.'

The Doctor hurried along the corridors and made his way to one of the entrances to the secret passage. He was reaching for the torch-holder when a guard stepped from behind a tapestry, holding a pike to his chest.

Ortron came around the corner flanked by more guards. 'You were warned not to attempt to leave the Citadel, Doctor, and you have disobeyed my command. Take him to the dungeon!'

Guards seized the Doctor's arms.

'Ortron, listen to me,' shouted the Doctor. 'You're making a grave mistake.'

Ortron smiled and stroked his beard. 'It is you who have made the mistake, Doctor—and it will be your last. Take him away!'

The guards bore the frantically struggling Doctor towards the dungeons.

6

The Intruder

Eckersley bent over the sonic cannon, checking the mechanism for signs of damage. To his relief, its period of abandonment seemed to have done it no harm.

A squad of guards stood by, waiting to drag the heavy machine back into the safety of the Citadel.

Eckersley and the guards were unaware of a party of miners watching them from the side tunnels. The group was led by Ettis. Gebek was there too, hoping to be able to exercise some sort of restraining influence.

'We're only just in time,' whispered Ettis. 'He's preparing to take the cannon back to the Citadel. Only he's left it too late.' He ducked down. 'Someone's coming.'

They saw Sarah come into the cavern and run up to Eckersley.

Eckersley looked up in surprise as Sarah approached. 'What are you doing here?'

'Looking for Gebek and the rebels. Have you seen them?'

'No, and I don't want to either. I had an idea they might try to steal my sonic cannon.' Eckersley patted the machine affectionately. 'She's still here though, safe and sound.'

In the nearby tunnel mouth Ettis hissed. 'Well, what are we waiting for? Let's attack!'

They began creeping forward . . .

'I wish to protest most strongly at the arrest of the Doctor,' said Alpha Centauri indignantly.

Ortron stood in his usual position, beside the throne, looming over the slender figure of Thalira.

'The Doctor was ordered to remain in the Citadel. He chose to disobey and must take the consequences.'

'Once again, you exceed your authority, Lord Ortron,' said Thalira icily. 'We ordered that the Doctor be allowed to continue his investigations.'

'Your Majesty, I myself heard him admit that he planned to contact the rebel leader Gebek.'

Thalira was silent, not daring to admit that the Doctor had been going to see Gebek at her request.

Alpha Centauri said, 'The Doctor is under the protection of the Federation.'

Ortron swung round on him. 'Is he, Ambassador? Is he indeed? Has he any official rank or position within the Federation?'

'The position of the Doctor is unique . . .'

'But you can at least produce his Federation identity documents?'

Alpha Centauri's tentacles flailed agitatedly. 'They seem to have been mislaid at the moment . . .' There had always been some doubt about the Doctor's exact identity and position, he reflected. Even on his first visit to Peladon he had appeared and disappeared mysteriously.

Ortron spread his hand. 'You see, Your Majesty. A nameless alien, with no status, no official existence!'

'Whoever the Doctor may be,' said Thalira bravely, 'we have chosen to give him our royal friendship and protection.'

'Then it is the duty of Your Majesty's loyal servants to protect her from her errors. The Doctor will remain in prison until his status is established. I shall issue orders for the arrest of his companion.'

'No, Ortron,' said Thalira fiercely. 'That you shall not do. The girl Sarah is my friend. She will be left at liberty.'

Having gained a major point, Ortron was prepared to concede a minor one. 'As Your Majesty wishes. Since the alien is only a female, she is of little importance . . .'

Thalira bit her lip, but did not reply. She was thinking of something Sarah had said, 'There's nothing "only" about being a female . . .'

The rebel attack had thrown the guards into confusion, and they fell back, running for cover.

Eckersley, however, leapt behind the controls of the sonic cannon and swung it round to cover the rebels.

The machine hummed with power, Eckersley depressed the muzzle and a string of explosions rocked the ground in front of the rebels. Eckersley grinned and looked down at Sarah, who was crouching beside the cannon. 'That'll teach them to pinch my equipment.'

But Sarah was looking over his shoulder. 'Eckersley, look out!'

Eckersley turned. Ettis had worked his way behind him in the fighting and was aiming a blaster straight at his head, from very close range. 'Do not move, Eckersley.'

Eckersley sighed and took his hands from the controls. 'Well, it was worth a try!' He jumped down from the machine, and stood looking on disconsolately as rebels attached ropes to the cannon and began dragging it across the cavern.

Sarah spotted Gebek and Preba looking on, and hurried up to them. 'I've got a message for you, Gebek, from the Doctor,' she whispered. 'The Queen wants you to come and see her—in secret.'

Gebek glanced round to see that no one was in earshot. There was only Preba, and he could be trusted to keep silent. 'It won't be easy. I'll come to the Citadel as soon as I can.'

Eckersley watched his sonic cannon disappear down a side tunnel. 'All right, Ettis, you win. What are you going to do with us?'

Gebek came over to join them. Before Ettis could speak he said roughly. 'Nothing. You can go.'

'We should keep them as hostages,' said Ettis.

Gebek shook his head. 'We don't need hostages—all we need is the machine. Now go—aliens!'

'Let's not argue with him,' said Sarah hastily. 'Let's get out of here.'

'I suppose you're right,' said Eckersley glumly, and allowed her to lead him away.

Not long afterwards, they were telling their story to Queen Thalira and Chancellor Ortron.

'So,' growled Ortron. 'Now the rebels have this weapon in their hands.'

'There wasn't much I could do,' said Eckersley matter-of-factly. 'The rebels had Federation blasters, and your guards didn't.'

'How dangerous is this device?' asked Thalira.

Eckersley frowned. 'Well, it wasn't designed as a weapon, Your Majesty, but it can be used as one. Properly handled and at full power, it could set off a sonic chain reaction that would destroy this Citadel.'

'The Federation troops will not be pleased to hear that news,' said Alpha Centauri worriedly.

'Federation troops?' growled Ortron. 'We want no alien troops on Peladon.'

Alpha Centauri bowed to the Queen. 'Forgive me, Your Majesty, I should have informed you earlier, but with all this confusion . . . The situation looked so dangerous I felt obliged to ask for Federation help.'

'But that's sure to make the miners fight,' said Sarah.

'The Doctor was of the same opinion,' admitted Alpha Centauri unhappily.

'Can't you send them back?'

'I fear not. It is a simple matter to send for Federation security troops. But once summoned, they cannot be recalled without a full enquiry by the Council.'

'Well, if they've got to come,' said Sarah thoughtfully, 'the thing to do is make sure they pack up and go away again as soon as possible. They'll only go if they're sure there's no real need for them. So if everything *seems* to be running smoothly . . . We must put on an act for them.'

'How can we do that?' demanded Ortron suspiciously.

Sarah smiled. 'Listen . . .'

The Doctor lounged against the bars of his cell, his mind busy with the possibility of escape. The cell consisted of a bare chamber, with no windows. Three walls were of solid rock, and the fourth made of iron bars, floor to ceiling, with a small gate set into them. On the far side of the bars was a gloomy corridor, patrolled by a guard with a drawn sword.

The guard came quite close to the bars at the end of his patrol, and as he passed the Doctor sneaked a long arm through the bars and tried to lift the keys from his belt. He didn't quite make it. The guard saw him and whirled round, slashing at the Doctor's hand with his sword. The Doctor snatched his hand back and the sword clashed against the bars. 'No need to be aggressive,' said the Doctor reproachfully. 'Can't blame me for trying, can you?'

The guard resumed his patrol, keeping a safe distance from the bars.

'What about a glass of water?' asked the Doctor hopefully.

The guard ignored him.

In the anteroom, Sarah was discussing her plan to restore apparent normality to Peladon with Alpha Centauri. 'Well, there you are—it ought to work.'

'A most excellent scheme,' agreed Alpha Centauri. 'Worthy of the Doctor himself.'

'At least old Ortron's agreed to co-operate. He doesn't want Federation troops on Peladon any more than the Doctor does. Which reminds me . . .' Sarah started to leave.

'Where are you going, Sarah?'

'To try and find this dungeon where they're holding the Doctor.'

'You are going to visit him?'

'No, I'm going to get him out!'

For once Sarah had a stroke of luck. She was hurrying along the Citadel corridors in what she hoped was the direction of the dungeons when she saw Gebek appear from behind a tapestry. 'How did you get here?'

'There are many secret ways into this Citadel. Where's the Doctor?'

'Ortron's had him thrown in the dungeons. I was just going to try to find him.'

'He'll be in the lower dungeons,' said Gebek.

'Which way is that? Can you take me there?'

'If they see you down there, they'll get suspicious. Probably lock you up with him. You go back to the others, and leave this to me.'

The Doctor was stretched out on his bunk, wondering where his guard had gone to, when he saw him reappear with a jug and a metal goblet. 'Ah, my glass of water at last.'

He watched the guard filling the goblet. 'I do believe it's wine. How very kind.'

64

The Doctor stretched out his hand. The guard raised the goblet to his own lips, and swigged it down, grinning at the Doctor.

Over the guard's shoulder, the Doctor caught a quick glimpse of Gebek lurking in the corridor.

As the guard put down the goblet, the Doctor called, 'I say, old chap, have you seen this?'

The guard looked. There was a gleaming metal coin in the Doctor's hand. Suddenly it vanished. The Doctor reached up and produced the coin from his own nose.

Fascinated, the guard moved forward. The coin vanished and the Doctor produced it from his ear.

By now Gebek was right behind the guard.

'Oh, there you are Gebek,' said the Doctor cheerfully.

The guard whirled round, and Gebek's big fist took him beneath the jaw.

Gebek caught him as he fell, lowered the body to the ground, snatched the keys from the man's belt, and released the Doctor. He dragged the body of the guard into the cell and locked him in. 'Sarah tells me the Queen wants to see me, Doctor. Shall we go to see her now?'

'If you don't mind, I'd like to take a look at the refinery. From what Sarah tells me, there's something very suspicious going on.'

With much sweating and cursing, the rebels, under Ettis's direction, had dragged the sonic cannon through a network of mountain tunnels up a steadily rising passage that emerged into a small cave on a neighbouring peak.

Ettis supervised the installation of the weapon. When everything was arranged to his satisfaction, he got behind the controls and sighted along the barrel at his target—the towering Citadel of Peladon.

Gebek was leading the Doctor on a short cut through the mine tunnels when they heard marching feet.

Ducking back into the shadows, they saw a group of miners being marched past by a squad of guards. 'They must be mad,' whispered Gebek. 'Miners won't work with guards standing over them. Treatment like this will drive them to rebellion, Doctor. And once those Federation troops arrive, my men will fight.'

'I believe you,' said the Doctor hurriedly. 'That's why we've got to sort out this Aggedor trickery before they arrive.'

Sarah, Eckersley and Alpha Centauri listened to the distorted crackling voice that came from the receiver in the communications room. It was harsh and military-sounding.

'Our ship is now in orbit around Peladon. Preliminary detachments will land by scout ship, close to the Citadel.'

'Your message received and understood,' replied Alpha Centauri nervously. 'We await your arrival.'

'Well, they're on their way,' said Sarah grimly.

Alpha Centauri said, 'The reponse is far quicker than I had expected.'

Eckersley grunted. 'Don't see how you hope to fool them for long.'

'With any luck, they won't be here for long,' Sarah pointed out. 'That's the whole idea.'

'Long enough to enable me to force Ortron to release the Doctor, I hope,' said Alpha Centauri fussily.

Sarah smiled. 'Don't worry about the Doctor—he can look after himself.'

The Doctor and Gebek came through an arch and found themselves before a smooth metal door set into the rock face. There was no light behind its glass panel.

'This is the place, Doctor,' said Gebek. 'But be careful. They say demons attack those who linger here.'

The Doctor smiled at this description of Eckersley's alarm system. 'Don't worry, old chap, we'll deal with the demons before we start.' He spotted a control panel high in the wall, and attacked it with his sonic screwdriver.

Eckersley was pacing up and down the control room. 'What worries me is, what are Ettis and his friends up to? What are they planning to do with my sonic cannon?'

'Maybe they just wanted to stop you using it,' said Sarah consolingly.

'Or use it for another bit of sabotage! I think I'll check the mine area on the monitors, maybe I can spot them.'

The entire mine area was covered by a system of automatic cameras. Eckersley went over to the appropriate console and began flicking up a series of pictures on the monitor screen. They showed mine gallery after mine gallery, corridor after corridor, junction after junction—all silent and deserted.

'The Federation troops will arrive at any moment,' twittered Alpha Centauri.

Eckersley got a picture of Ortron and an escort of guards marching along the central mine gallery. 'There's Ortron now.'

Eckersley cut to another picture and gave a whistle of astonishment. 'Look at this, here's your friend the Doctor. The old devil seems to be on the loose again already.'

The monitor showed the Doctor and Gebek outside the refinery door.

'Well, well, well, who'd have thought it,' said Sarah innocently.

Eckersley peered at the monitor. 'That's Gebek with

him. What are those two up to?'

Alpha Centauri came to look at the screen. 'The Doctor appears to be helping Gebek to break into the refinery,' he observed mildly.

'What!' Eckersley headed for the door. 'We'll see about that!'

Sarah ran to bar his way. 'No wait. The Doctor and I think the Aggedor trick may be being worked from the refinery.'

'Well, of all the daft ideas!'

'If we're wrong, there's no harm done, is there? The Doctor won't harm your precious machinery, I promise you.'

'Maybe not,' said Eckersley bluntly. 'But if the Doctor's right and if he gets into the refinery—what's he going to find waiting for him?'

In the mine's main gallery, Chancellor Ortron was addressing a captive audience—a large group of miners, dragged here from their hovels at sword point.

Ortron raised his voice. 'Listen to me, all of you!' An uneasy silence fell. 'As a result of recent outbreaks of violence, Federation troops are about to land on Peladon.'

There was a roar of anger. 'Don't think that'll save you, Ortron!' someone shouted.

Ortron raised his voice again. 'I did not send for them, I want them here no more than you do. Our only hope is to convince them that their presence is not needed. And the only way to do that is to return the mines to normal working.'

There was another roar of protest.

'I appeal to you, for the sake of Peladon,' shouted Ortron. 'Return to work. When the Federation troops have gone, we can settle our differences without alien interference. I promise you a fair hearing for all your complaints.'

There was a murmur of talk as the miners discussed the situation amongst themselves. Then an old miner stepped forward. 'All right, Ortron. We'll trust you—this time. Come on, lads, back to work. Find the others and tell them.'

Suddenly a bright light shone from the rock wall and the glowing shape of Aggedor materialised. A beam of light shot from the statue, and the body of the old miner glowed brightly then disappeared.

Merging into one panic-stricken mob, Ortron, his guards and the miners fled down the tunnels.

The Doctor had neutralised the alarm and was at work on the refinery door.

'Listen,' said Gebek. 'I can hear shouting, people running. They're coming this way!'

'Don't worry, old chap,' said the Doctor absently. 'I'll have this open in a jiffy. Ah, here we are.'

He cross-connected a circuit, and the door swung open.

The Doctor heard Gebek's gasp of horror and looked up.

A terrifying figure stood in the refinery doorway.

It was immensely tall, covered with green scaly hide that was ridged and plated like that of a crocodile. Its helmet-like head showed a lipless scaly-skinned lower jaw, and its two huge eyes were like blank, black, glass screens. Its huge hands were like crude, powerful clamps. One of them was raised, pointing menacingly at the Doctor. It was an Ice Warrior.

7

The Ice Warriors

The Doctor stared at the giant figure in astonishment. He had seen Ice Warriors before, here on Peladon, and long ago on the planet Earth. But he hadn't expected to meet one here, in the doorway of the supposedly disused refinery.

The Ice Warrior strode forward. 'Do not move,' it hissed. 'You are my prisoners.'

Sarah and Eckersley and Alpa Centauri watched the scene on their monitor.

'What is that thing?' whispered Sarah.

'They are Martians,' said Alpha Centauri. 'Your friend the Doctor calls them Ice Warriors. He claims to have encountered them long ago on the planet Earth. It is unfortunate that the security section chose to send a detachment of Martian troops to Peladon. They are ruthless militarists, concerned only with results. It will not be easy to negotiate with them.'

Ettis and his rebels were holding yet another council of war in their secret hide – out. They were discussing Gebek. Despite Ettis's recent ascendancy, Gebek was still a much-loved leader amongst the miners. Young Preba—who had easily eluded the guards, as he had predicted—was one of Gebek's keenest supporters. 'I tell you he's gone back to the Citadel. The alien girl brought him a message, said the Queen wanted a secret meeting.'

'And he believed her?' said Ettis scornfully. 'Then he walked into a trap.'

'Maybe he did,' said Preba. 'The question is, what are we going to do about it?'

'Nothing. Gebek's beyond help now.'

'You're talking as if he was already dead.'

Ettis shrugged. 'Dead, or a prisoner of Ortron, or of the Federation. What's the difference?'

'So you're just going to abandon him? Perhaps it would suit you better, Ettis, if Gebek never came back.'

'Of course not. But what can we do?'

'Rescue him.'

'But the Federation troops have landed!'

Preba pointed to the blaster in Ettis's belt. 'Ah, but we're not afraid of Federation troops now, are we, Ettis? Not now we have our new weapons.'

Ettis realised that he had been outmanoeuvred, and attempted to save as much prestige as he could from the situation. 'Very well, I suppose we must risk our lives to save Gebek from the consequences of his own stupidity.' He stood up. 'I only hope you think the price is worth it. Come on!'

Queen Thalira was on her throne, with all the notables of Peladon assembled around her. Dominating the room was the towering green figure of Azaxyr, Commander of the Federation security troops, all Martians like himself. The green-scaled giants seemed to be everywhere in the Citadel, guarding the throne room and patrolling the corridors outside.

Sarah was studying Azaxyr in fascination. There were a number of physical differences between the Commander and the other warriors, such as Sskel, his giant henchman, the Ice Warrior who had captured the Doctor. Although equally large, Azaxyr was built on slenderer, more graceful lines than his tank-like troops. He moved more easily, and in particular his mouth and jaw were differently made, less of a piece with the helmet-like head. While the other Ice Warriors grunted and hissed in monosyllables, Azaxyr spoke clearly and fluently, though there was still the characteristic Martian sibilance in his voice.

She had mentioned these differences to the Doctor at the beginning of the meeting and the Doctor had whispered, 'Azaxyr is a Martian aristocrat, Sarah, almost a different species from the ordinary warriors. Just as much of a ruthless killer—but highly intelligent as well. Makes him even more dangerous!'

Azaxyr was demonstrating that intelligence now, together with a certain sardonic humour, as he summed up the results of that first council.

'So,' he hissed, 'let us see what has emerged. Chancellor Ortron says the miners have rebelled against their rightful rulers. Gebek says the nobles have cheated his people out of their rights. The Chancellor says the Doctor is a spy and saboteur, the Ambassador swears that he is an old and valued friend. Gebek says his god appears to his people because he is angry, the Doctor is sure that these appearances are caused by trickery.'

'An excellent summing-up, Commander Azaxyr,' said the Doctor cheerfully. 'You'd have made a very good judge.'

'You forget, Doctor, I am your judge. Your jury and your executioner too, perhaps.' Azaxyr turned to Eckersley, who was lounging casually against the wall. 'Only our engineer here says nothing and accuses nobody.'

Eckersley shrugged. 'None of my business, is it? I came here to mine trisilicate, and I just wish people would let me get on with it.'

'Excellent!' hissed Azaxyr. 'A splendid example to

you all.' He stepped up onto the royal dais, dominating the room effortlessly. 'Now, listen to me, all of you. I am not concerned with the internal squabbles of Peladon. One thing concerns me, and one thing only—that the Federation has the trisilicate it needs to win this war.'

'But it's the situation on Peladon that's stopping you from getting the trisilicate,' pointed out the Doctor. 'You've got to be concerned with it, like it or not!'

'Then let me offer a simple solution. Gebek, your miners will return to work at once. They will work under the supervision of my troops and of armed guards, which you, Chancellor, will supply.'

'My men are united,' said Gebek. 'We shall defy you!'

Astonishingly, Ortron came to stand by his side. 'And I will not turn my troops on their fellow Peladonians at the orders of an alien power.'

'He was willing enough to do it on his own account,' whispered Sarah.

The Doctor smiled. 'That's different.'

Azaxyr had his own way of crushing opposition. 'Sskel!'

The towering figure stepped forward from the doorway. 'Yes, Commander?'

'You are ready to select hostages?'

'Yes, Commander.'

'Good!' Azaxyr turned to Gebek and Ortron. 'Until the miners return to work, a certain number of hostages will be executed every day.'

Ettis was assembling his commando squad by the entrance to the Citadel. 'Everyone here? Good. Once Gebek is safe we give our ultimatum to the Federation. Unless the Federation troops leave at once, and all our other demands are agreed, we will destroy the Citadel.'

'As you say, Ettis,' agreed Preba. 'But no ultimatum till we're sure Gebek is safe.'

They moved into the Citadel corridors.

73

As they emerged, a palace guard appeared, and Ettis and his men jumped him immediately.

Preba held a blaster to the man's head. 'Where is Gebek, our leader? Is he in the dungeons? Speak or die!'

'He is in the throne room, with the others,' gasped the guard.

Preba reversed his blaster and clubbed him down.

Leaving the body where it fell, the rebels crept towards the throne room.

Azaxyr's chilling ultimatum had roused a storm of protest. 'You are exceeding your authority,' said Queen Thalira.

Even Alpha Centauri nerved himself to say, 'The Federation simply does not use such methods.'

'Not in time of peace, Ambassador,' hissed Azaxyr. 'But this is war.' He turned to the Queen. 'I assure you, Your Majesty, I have been authorised to use *any* method to secure our supplies of trisilicate.'

Sarah nudged the Doctor. 'Can't you do something?'

The Doctor stepped forward. 'Suppose these terror methods don't work, Commander—what then?'

'We shall place the entire planet under martial law, bring in Federation miners and equipment, and mine the trisilicate ourselves.'

'We shall never allow that, Commander,' said Thalira.

Gebek moved to stand beside the throne. 'If you try, every man, woman and child on Peladon will oppose you.'

The Doctor smiled. 'See how fiercely they unite against you, Commander. It's no easy matter to hold down a hostile planet—not if you're fighting a war at the same time.'

'Then our space fleet will blast this planet to dust,' hissed Azaxyr furiously. 'If we cannot have the trisilicate, neither will Galaxy Five . . .'

The Doctor said, 'I just thought you ought to know what you're up against, Commander. You were sent here for trisilicate, and now you are reduced to threatening to destroy its leading source. Do you think your superiors will be pleased?'

Azaxyr drew a deep, hissing breath. 'Naturally we should prefer a more peaceful solution. Let us hope there will be no need to contemplate extreme measures . . .'

There was a scuffle in the doorway. Preba and a small group of miners burst in, blasters in their hands. 'Quick, come with us, Gebek. The rest of you, don't move!'

Before Gebek could respond, Azaxyr hissed. 'Destroy them!'

Instantly the Ice Warrior guards opened fire. They stretched out their hands with the strange built-in sonic guns, and fired. The rebels' bodies seemed to pulse and quiver, and then fell dead to the ground. Not one of the rebels had time to fire a shot. It was not so much a battle as a massacre.

Only Ettis survived. He turned and sped from the room, ran frantically along the corridor, and was soon safe behind the tapestry.

The last of the miners' bodies twitched and lay still.

Azaxyr turned to the Queen, who crouched white-faced on her throne. 'My apologies, Your Majesty. This—demonstration was forced on me. Let us hope that another will not be necessary. Sskel, take the Doctor and his friend to the communications room. Ambassador, Engineer Eckersley, you will accompany us.'

Azaxyr stalked out, and Sskel herded the others after him. Thalira, Ortron and Gebek stood stunned, amidst the littered bodies of the miners.

In a low angry voice Ortron said, 'We shall be revenged!'

Azaxyr looked thoughtfully at the Doctor. 'I am not sure what to make of you, Doctor. I think it would be safer to accept Chancellor Ortron's theory and have you executed as a spy and saboteur. Something tells me it would be safer.'

'You can't do that,' said Sarah furiously. 'We're not under your authority.'

'Must I again remind you—here on Peladon, I am the law. Yes, Doctor, on the whole I am inclined to order your immediate execution. Sskel!'

The Ice Warrior raised his gun.

'Don't I even get a trial?' asked the Doctor indignantly.

'Doctor, that was your trial.' hissed Azaxyr.

The Doctor said calmly. 'Didn't you say you wanted to find a peaceful solution?'

'If possible, yes.'

'Then you'd be very foolish to polish off the one man who can help you get it!'

'You, Doctor?'

'Me!' confirmed the Doctor. 'Gebek is the key to the whole situation, and I happen to be the only one he trusts.'

'That's true,' said Sarah hurriedly. 'The Doctor saved Gebek's life and they've been working together ever since.'

Azaxyr's blank eyes swung round to Alpha Centauri. 'Ambassador?'

'There is most certainly a close association between them.'

'Engineer Eckersley?'

Eckersley hesitated. 'Well, I suppose it's worth a try. If the Doctor could persuade Gebek to get the men working again . . .'

Azaxyr considered for what seemed a very long moment. 'Very well, Doctor, you may attempt to persuade your friend Gebek to see reason.'

Sskel lowered his sonic gun.

'However,' continued Azaxyr, 'if you fail, I shall be forced to fall back on my original plan. And I assure you, Doctor, you will be the first hostage to be executed.' Azaxyr turned to Eckersley. 'Is the refinery in working order?'

'Theoretically. It's on shutdown at the moment.'

'Take me there. I shall make a full inspection. There must be no delays in refining once production has started.'

Eckersley headed for the door. 'There won't be any delays my end, Commander. You get me the trisilicate, and I'll refine it!'

As Azaxyr and Eckersley left, Sarah said disgustedly, 'Listen to that Eckersley. As long as he gets his wretched ore to refine, he doesn't care how it's done, or who suffers.'

'It's called the professional attitude,' said the Doctor.

Sarah sighed. 'I wish we could just go home, Doctor.'

'And leave our friends on Peladon in the lurch? Besides we'd never get to the TARDIS, Azaxyr would see to that.'

'I suppose you're right,' said Sarah gloomily. She glanced out into the corridor. Sskel had been left on guard, and his shadow fell into the room. The distorted shape reminded Sarah of something. 'Doctor!' she said excitedly.

'What is it?'

'You remember that shape I told you I saw behind the door in the refinery, the first time I went there? It was Azaxyr I'm certain of it.'

'That is impossible,' said Alpha Centauri. 'The Commander and his troops have just arrived.'

'If Sarah's right,' said the Doctor thoughtfully, 'then Azaxyr and Sskel have been here all along. And that means Azaxyr isn't acting on behalf of the Federation. He's up to some game of his own.' He looked at Alpha

77

Centauri. 'Don't you think that Ice Warrior force arrived with amazing speed? Suppose the ship was here all along, orbiting the planet, with Azaxyr and Sskel up to no good in the refinery. They could have intercepted your message to the Federation and pretended to answer it!'

Alpha Centauri was horrified. 'But this is appalling. It is high treason against the Federation.'

'Yes, it is, isn't it,' said the Doctor thoughtfully. 'I think I'd better go and have my chat with Gebek, before Azaxyr changes his mind about my execution.' He headed for the door.

The massive form of Sskel appeared, barring his way. 'Where are you going?'

'Your Commander says I'm to persuade Gebek to co-operate. I can't persuade him if I can't talk to him, can I? Out of the way, old chap.'

Sskel moved reluctantly aside, and the Doctor slipped past him and out into the corridor. Sskel followed.

Alpha Centauri hurried over to the communications console. 'Commander Azaxyr's conduct is highly reprehensible. I shall report him to the Federation immediately. He will be recalled at once. He will be severely punished!'

Sarah said thoughtfully. 'The Doctor was saying how intelligent Azaxyr was. It's a wonder he didn't think of that possibility himself.'

Alpha Centauri's tentacles flew over the controls. 'This is the Federation Ambassador on Peladon. I wish to send an urgent message to Federation HQ.'

Nothing came from the machine but a high-pitched whine, broken up by static. 'The call is being jammed,' whispered Alpha Centauri. 'It's Azaxyr's ship, in orbit around the planet!'

Sarah said grimly. 'So he did think of it after all!'

'He's cut us off from communication with the Federation,' whispered Alpha Centauri. 'We're trapped!'

8

The Madman

By the time the Doctor returned to the throne room, Sskel at his heels, the bodies of the slaughtered miners had been taken away.

Ortron and Gebek were huddled protectively around the throne, talking in low voices to Queen Thalira.

The Queen looked up as the Doctor entered. 'Doctor!'

The Doctor bowed. 'Your Majesty.' He hurried over to the little group around the throne—to his relief, Sskel remained on guard in the doorway. 'Listen, Gebek, there's not much time. I want you to persuade the miners to go back to work.'

It was Ortron who answered him. 'Never. Gebek and I are united. We shall fight the invaders together.'

'Chancellor Ortron is right,' growled Gebek. 'From the death of the first hostage, it will be war!'

Thalira leaned forward on the throne. 'As you can see, Doctor, our people would sooner die than be enslaved.'

'Nice to see all the Peladonions on the same side for once,' said the Doctor ironically. He lowered his voice. 'I don't mean *really* co-operate. I want the miners to pretend to co-operate. It'll save unnecessary deaths, and give me a chance to deal with the Ice Warriors. Will they do it?'

Gebek said slowly, 'They might—if they understood what was happening.'

'You'll have to make them understand, won't you?

Here's what I suggest . . .'

Gebek looked at the grim suspicious faces all around him. Like Ortron earlier, he was talking to a captive audience, miners' leaders rounded up and brought to the main gallery by the guards. This time there was the additional threat of the Ice Warriors, their giant green forms interspersed with Ortron's men.

Gebek drew a deep breath. It was going to be a difficult speech since almost every word had to carry a double meaning. 'Friends, you all know me. I'm one of you and I always will be. However it may sound to you, what I say now won't alter that, so listen carefully.'

The miners looked at each other in puzzlement. Gebek was a blunt and plain-spoken man, like themselves. It wasn't like him to drop obscure hints. Something was up . . .

'I'm here because Commander Azaxyr trusts me. He knows that you trust me too, and that you'll do what I tell you—just as we've always done what Chancellor Ortron tells us. In spite of all that's happened I want you to persuade the miners to go back to work, to co-operate with Federation troops.'

A puzzled silence greeted his words. Gebek raised his voice. 'I've discussed things with our friend the Chancellor, and he's in full agreement. We are going to co-operate with Commander Azaxyr in the same way we've been co-operating with Chancellor Ortron! You remember how we co-operated over the use of the sonic cannon? How we co-operated over the Federation armoury? Well, that's the kind of co-operation we're going to give Commander Azaxyr and his Federation troops. *Now* do you understand me?'

There was a rumble of assent from the miners. One or two of them had broad grins on their faces.

The Doctor leaned forward. 'Congratulations, Gebek, I think they've got the message.'

'My congratulations, Doctor,' hissed Azaxyr. 'Most satisfactory. The miners are back at work, and the stocks of trisilicate ore are building up. Eckersley informs me that the refinery will soon be ready to start work. You have done well.'

'Thank you,' said the Doctor modestly. They were walking along the corridor to the communications room. 'I take it my death sentence has been lifted?'

'Let us say, suspended. You will live while you are useful.'

'Well, that's something, I suppose!'

'I still do not trust you, Doctor. I trust you realise that your only chance of survival lies in full co-operation?'

'Of course. Survival is something I've always been very keen on.'

Azaxyr came to a halt outside the communications room door. 'Very well, Doctor. You will be confined to the Federation quarters while I decide upon your eventual fate.'

Azaxyr swept on his way, and the Doctor went into the communications room, where an anxious Sarah was waiting for him.

'So much for phase one,' said the Doctor cheerfully. 'Time for phase two, I think.'

He crossed to the bank of consoles that controlled conditions in the mine.

'Be careful, Doctor, Azaxyr still doesn't trust you. If he so much as suspects you're double-crossing him, he'll kill you.'

'My dear Sarah, Azaxyr will kill me anyway, as soon as I'm no longer useful to him.' The Doctor's hands were busy at the controls.

'What are you doing?'

'Making things hot for Azaxyr's men.' The Doctor grinned mischievously. 'The one thing Ice Warriors can't stand is heat!'

Sickened and horrified at the massacre of his men, Ettis had fled through the mines and hid himself in one of the remote disused galleries. He lay there in the darkness sobbing. Over and over again he saw his men twist and fall beneath the Ice Warriors' sonic guns.

Eventually curiosity drove him from hiding, and he made his way cautiously towards the major galleries.

To his astonishment he came upon a party of miners working at the rock face, an Ice Warrior guard looming over them.

There was a sub-gallery close to the working party and Ettis concealed himself in the entrance.

He gave a low hiss, and the nearest miner looked up.

Ettis beckoned and the miner slipped away into the gallery. 'Ettis! We all thought you'd been killed.'

'What's been happening? Why is everyone working.'

'Gebek told us to. Came down here and made a speech to the section leaders, said everyone should co-operate.'

'I knew it. He's a traitor!'

'No, you don't understand, it's all a trick. Gebek has a plan.'

'Gebek has betrayed us,' muttered Ettis. 'Gone over to the other side.'

Suddenly Ettis knew what he must do. 'Well, I've got a plan of my own. I've got the sonic cannon hidden in a cave overlooking the Citadel. I'm going to destroy it, blow the whole place up.'

'But the Queen's there. You'd be killing the Queen! And your own people too. If you bring the Citadel down on top of us, half the mines will cave in.'

'Kill them all,' muttered Ettis fiercely. 'Queen, Chancellor, guards, traitors like Gebek. It's worth it to slaughter all the Federation troops—the way they slaughtered us!'

The miner looked hard at him. 'You're mad, Ettis. I'm going to tell Gebek.'

Ettis snatched up a chunk of rock. 'You'll tell no one,' he snarled, and smashed the rock down on his fellow miner's head.

Leaving the body crumpled on the floor, Ettis hurried away.

The Doctor studied the flickering dials. 'Should be warming up nicely now.'

'What will it do to the Ice Warriors?'

'If they don't get out of the mines soon, they'll get groggier and groggier, until they collapse . . .'

The bulk of the miners were chipping away at the main rock face, supervised by a line of Ice Warrior guards. Gebek hurried along the gallery. 'Well done, lads, keep it up.' He moved closer to the guard Captain and whispered. 'Not long now. Are your men ready?'

'They're ready—as soon as you give the signal . . .'

Sskel lumbered towards them, his movements even heavier and more awkward than usual. 'It is hot,' he hissed laboriously. 'Why is it so hot?'

'Because we're underground,' said Gebek innocently. 'It's always warm down here.' He winked at the guard Captain. 'We have a saying on Peladon—if you can't stand the heat, stay out of the mine!'

In the throne room, a nervous Alpha Centauri was in low-voiced conference with Queen Thalira and her Chancellor.

'As soon as Gebek gives the signal, our guards will

join the miners in an attack on the Federation troops.'

'The plan is a dangerous one,' said Thalira. 'Will it work?'

Alpha Centauri's tentacles rippled nervously. 'The plan was conceived by the Doctor—and he has fought the Ice Warriors before.'

They fell silent as Azaxyr strode in the throne room. 'A conference, Your Majesty?'

'I have just been informing the Ambassador that I intend to make formal complaint to the Federation concerning your violation of the sovereignty of our planet. I demand immediate communication with the Federation Council.'

'For the moment that is impossible,' said Azaxyr smoothly. 'This whole planet is under a communications seal until the emergency is over.'

'But surely it is over now? The miners are back at work are they not?'

'I think we shall wait a little longer,' hissed Azaxyr. 'This settlement has come too easily. I distrust it.'

Gebek was watching the Ice Warrior guards closely. One of them staggered, and almost fell. Gebek leaped into the centre of the long gallery. 'Now!' he shouted. 'Attack now!'

Gebek and the guard Captain leaped on the reeling Ice Warrior and thrust hard. The giant green figure staggered and crashed to the ground.

All over the galleries, guards and miners combined to attack the enfeebled Ice Warriors.

The battle for Peladon had begun.

The Doctor and Sarah watched the confused struggle on the monitor. Even when weakened by the heat, the Ice Warriors were still terrifyingly strong. It took several

Peladonians to bring one down. Once down the Ice Warriors found it hard to rise again, rolling to and fro on their backs, like stranded turtles.

The Peladonians attacked them with swords and spears and picks and chunks of rock, but the Ice Warriors were astonishingly hard to kill. Even when overturned, they were dangerous, flailing around them with their mighty limbs and firing wildly around them. Many a Peladonian was smashed down by a savage blow from a massive armoured hand, or died screaming in the blast of a sonic gun.

'Time we were going, I think,' said the Doctor. 'We'd better get down there.'

Sarah shuddered, and looked away from the screen. 'It doesn't look very safe.'

'It won't be very safe up here when Azaxyr learns what we've been up to.'

'What about the Ice Warrior on the door?'

The Doctor went to the door and called, 'Come quickly, there's trouble in the mines.'

The Ice Warrior lumbered into the room, and stood staring at the monitor screen. The Doctor and Sarah slipped around behind the Ice Warrior, and out of the door.

As they ran down the corridor, Sarah said, 'He'll go straight to Azaxyr and report.'

'That's right. The more men Azaxyr sends down to the mines, the better for us. They'll be at a disadvantage down there.'

'And what happens when they're all down there. Tell me your plan.'

'Gebek leads a party of Peladonians up here and recaptures the Citadel. Then we send a fake message to Azaxyr's ship, get it to land, capture that, switch off the jamming system and send a message to the Federation for help—the real Galactic Federation, not Azaxyr's band of renegades.'

Sarah looked at him admiringly. 'Quite the little Napoleon, aren't we?'

Slowly but surely the battle in the mines was swinging in the Peladonians' favour. Sskel and a number of other Ice Warriors had realised what was going on and were fighting their way back towards the Citadel.

Gebek was hurrying past a sub-gallery to check up on the situation around the Citadel when he heard a feeble voice call, 'Gebek!'

He looked in the sub-gallery and saw a miner trying to crawl towards him.

Gebek ran and knelt beside him. 'It's all right, I'm here. Were you wounded in the fighting?'

Feebly the miner shook his head. 'It was Ettis.'

'Ettis attacked you?'

'He's gone mad. He's got the sonic cannon in a cave . . . going to blow up the Citadel . . .'

Gebek jumped up. 'I must go and stop him. I'll send you help as soon as I can.'

As Gebek came out into the gallery he saw the Doctor and Sarah running towards him.

'How's it going, Gebek?' asked the Doctor.

'Not too badly. The battle's moved toward the surface. The Ice Warriors are trying to escape. Doctor, listen, Ettis has got the sonic cannon in a cave overlooking the Citadel. He plans to blow the whole place up. I've got to stop him.'

'No, Gebek, we need you here. I'll deal with Ettis.'

'You don't know how to find him.'

'Then tell me!'

The Doctor listened carefully as Gebek gave him directions how to find the tunnel that connected with the neighbouring peak. 'All right, I'll find it.'

Gebek handed over his sword. 'Take this, you may need it.'

'Thanks. Look after Sarah for me, will you?'

The Doctor turned and sprinted off down the gallery.

Abandoned again, thought Sarah bitterly. Gebek led her to the sub-gallery. 'You stay here and see if you can help him. I'll send help as soon as I can.'

Gebek hurried off, and Sarah was left alone with the wounded man. She knelt down beside him. His face was pale and his breathing shallow. There didn't seem to be anything she could do for him. Slipping off her jacket, Sarah folded it into a pillow, and slipped it gently beneath the wounded man's head.

Somewhere nearby she could here the yells of angry men, and the occasional screams of the dying.

She settled down to wait.

Suddenly a shadow loomed over her, and she looked up to see a huge terrifying form. It was Sskel.

'You are my prisoner,' he hissed. 'You will guide me to the surface.'

A clamp-like hand closed over her arm.

In his cave, Ettis was carefully lining up the sonic cannon with the base of the Citadel. He smiled in anticipation at the thought of the honeycombed mountain crumbling beneath the sonic beam, of the great Citadel of Peladon tumbling down into the valley below. It would be a splendid spectacle.

Azaxyr and Alpha Centauri were watching the battle on the monitor, when Sskel thrust Sarah into the communications room.

Alpha Centauri bustled towards her. 'Sarah! Are you all right?'

Commander Azaxyr thrust him aside and bore down on Sarah. 'Ssso! Where is the Doctor?'

The Doctor struggled up a long winding tunnel and emerged at last into the cave, where Ettis was beginning the power build-up on the sonic cannon. 'Ettis!' he yelled. 'Stay away from that thing!'

Ettis laughed wildly. 'I'm going to blow up the Citadel, kill all those Federation butchers.'

'Most of the Ice Warriors aren't even in the Citadel now, they're in the mines. The people of Peladon are fighting them, Ettis, miners and soldiers together. Fighting them and winning! If you use that cannon, you'll be killing your Queen and a lot of your own people.'

For a moment Ettis hesitated, then the madness returned to his eyes. 'I don't believe you, it's another trick. You've sold out, like Gebek and all the others!'

He bent over the controls.

The Doctor climbed up onto the cannon and tried to pull him away.

Ettis snatched the sword from his belt and aimed a savage cut at the Doctor's head.

The Doctor parried with Gebek's sword. Ettis slashed at him again and again, driving the Doctor back by the sheer fury of his blows.

'I tell you, the Doctor is trying to save all our lives,' said Sarah fiercely. 'One of the rebels has a sonic cannon trained on the Citadel. He's going to blow this whole place up unless the Doctor can stop him.'

'Indeed,' said Azaxyr calmly. 'We pinpointed the position of the sonic gun some time ago. We have it under observation now.' He adjusted controls on the monitor, and the scene in the mines was replaced by a view of the neighbouring peak. Azaxyr made more adjustments, and the camera zoomed into a close-up of the cave. They could see the sonic cannon aimed directly at them, with the Doctor and Ettis fighting fiercely around its base.

'It appears you are telling the truth,' hissed Azaxyr. For a moment he watched the fight with professional interest. 'The Doctor fights well.'

Alpha Centauri watched the scene in horror. 'Ettis appears deranged. What if he overcomes the Doctor?'

'Do not distress yourself, Ambassador,' hissed Azaxyr. 'I have taken the precaution of setting the sonic cannon's self-destruct circuit by remote control. Should anyone try to fire it, the cannon will blow itself up!'

He sat back to watch the struggle.

The Doctor was fighting defensively, handicapped by the fact that he didn't want to kill his opponent if he could avoid it.

Ettis had no such inhibitions, and he slashed and cut and thrust with a madman's energy.

With a final brilliant parry, the Doctor sent Ettis's sword flying from his hand.

The Doctor stepped back. 'Give in, Ettis I don't want to hurt you.'

With a scream of rage, Ettis leaped straight at the Doctor, knocking his sword arm aside, and felling him with a savage blow to the temple.

The Doctor fell dazed, and Ettis sprang behind the controls of the sonic cannon. He reached for the firing mechanism . . . With a blinding flash of light, the cannon blew up.

9

The Return of Aggedor

The little mountain cave was filled with dust and smoke. Except for a few twisted fragments of metal, the sonic cannon had completely disappeared.

Of Ettis and the Doctor, there was no sign at all.

Sarah looked up from the monitor in horror. 'The Doctor's dead, Azaxyr—and it's all your fault. You killed him!'

'In immobilising the cannon, I was merely defending the safety of the Citadel. The death of the Doctor was merely a side-effect.' Azaxyr switched off the monitor.

Sarah said fiercely, 'You still haven't won, you know. The rebels control the mines—and you can't fight them down there because of the heat.'

'Not so,' hissed Azaxyr. 'Once I realised the Doctor's scheme, I ordered Eckersley to return the heating controls to normal. We simply have to wait for the temperature to fall.'

'You still won't get your trisilicate, will you? Gebek and his miners will never give up those tunnels.'

'Again you underestimate me. Engineer Eckersley, I understand there is a ventilation system in the mines.'

'That's right. It's controlled from the refinery.'

Azaxyr turned to Sarah. 'The miners can live without heat—but not without air. Eckersley, you will go to the refinery and reverse the ventilation system, so that air is sucked *from* the tunnels.'

'Eckersley, don't do it,' begged Sarah. 'If you drive those miners from the tunnels, they'll all be massacred. Azaxyr's completely ruthless, he's already caused the death of the Doctor.'

'Perhaps the Doctor was too dangerous to live,' hissed Azaxyr.

Eckersley said awkwardly, 'Look, Sarah, I'm sorry about the Doctor, believe me. But I warned him not to interfere in local politics. I don't intend to make the same mistakes.'

Eckersley went out of the communications room.

'Sskel, take the female alien to the throne room with the others,' ordered Azaxyr. As Sarah was led away, he bore down on the quailing Alpha Centauri. 'Now, Ambassador, we have work to do. I have decided to reorganise the administration of this planet on more efficient lines. I shall require your help.'

The Doctor recovered consciousness at the top of the access tunnel, where his unconscious body had been thrown by the blast. Apart from a few minor bruises, he seemed quite unhurt. If you had to be caught in an explosion, he thought, perhaps it was actually a help to be knocked out.

He searched the rubble-strewn cave, but found no trace of Ettis. Presumably his body had been thrown the other way, over the edge of the cave to the valley below. In any event, the Citadel of Peladon was unharmed. Its black towers and battlements reared up as impressively as ever, crowning the peak of Mount Megeshra, on the other side of the valley.

The Doctor turned and ran down the long tunnel that led to the mines.

The journey was a long and weary one. At the point where the tunnel rejoined the mine galleries, the Doctor collapsed panting on a chunk of rock, for a much-needed rest.

He heard footsteps coming towards him and looked up to see Gebek. 'I was just coming to help you, Doctor. You stopped him then?'

'Well, something did, the whole gun blew up when he fired. How's the battle going?'

'Not too well, I'm afraid. We drove the Ice Warriors out of the mines, but we couldn't break through to the Citadel. Now the temperature's dropping again. What's worse, the men say the air in the lower galleries is going stale.'

'They've probably switched off the ventilation system.'

'If the air goes, Doctor, we'll be forced to the upper levels—with Ice Warriors waiting at every exit.'

'Where's the ventilation controlled from?'

'The refinery.'

'You'd better take me there, so I can switch the ventilation back on. Where's Sarah?' Gebek was silent. 'Answer me, man—where is she?'

'I left her looking after the miner Ettis attacked. When I came back for her, he was dead, and she'd gone. I'm sorry, Doctor, but with a battle going on . . . I did my best.'

'Yes, of course, it wasn't your fault, it was mine for bringing her. Don't worry, we'll find her. We'd better get moving.'

In the throne room the Queen was doing her best to comfort Sarah, who seemed almost stunned by grief. 'We will never forget him, Sarah,' she said gently. 'He was a true friend to Peladon. His name will always be honoured.'

'I still can't believe he's dead,' said Sarah dully. 'He was the most *alive* person I've ever met.'

Ortron said gruffly. 'Perhaps he escaped somehow. There is always a chance.'

Sarah tried to smile. 'That's the sort of thing the Doctor used to say. "There's always a chance . . . while there's life—" ' She broke off and turned away.

Alpha Centauri entered the throne room, scuttling nervously past the Ice Warrior on guard at the entrance. 'Your Majesty, I have just had a most exhausting meeting with Commander Azaxyr. We have been discussing his future rule of this planet.'

'His rule?' said Ortron angrily. 'Queen Thalira rules on Peladon.'

'From now on, she rules in name only. Azaxyr plans to extend his martial law over the whole of Peladon. All able-bodied citizens will be conscripted to work in the trisilicate mines. He intends to gut the planet, as rapidly as possible.'

'My people will not submit to this,' said Queen Thalira fiercely.

'Your people will have little choice,' said Alpha Centauri sadly. 'Azaxyr's Ice Warriors will see to that!'

'Surely the Federation will not approve such ruthless methods?' asked Ortron.

'They will never know, Lord Ortron. Azaxyr does not serve the Federation. He is a renegade, acting from motives of his own.'

'So if we could get a message out to the real Federation,' said Sarah. 'Tell them what Azaxyr's up to . . .'

'I have already tried,' said Alpha Centauri dejectedly. 'Azaxyr has blocked all the communication circuits . . .' Suddenly he broke off. 'The distress beacon! I could activate the spatial distress beacon.'

'Can we use it to send a message?'

'I fear not. It's only purpose is to send a powerful signal on a pre-set emergency frequency—a sort of automatic call for help.'

Sarah nodded understandingly. 'A kind of SOS.' She

jumped up. 'We'll try it. Was the communications room guarded when you left?'

'No. The room was empty.'

Sarah nodded towards the guard at the door. 'Then all we've got to do is get past our green and scaly friend there.'

Unexpectedly Queen Thalira joined in. 'We must lure him from the doorway. He moves too slowly to prevent our escape once we are past him.'

'Our escape, Your Majesty?' said Ortron in surprise.

'We intend to join the rebels in the mines.'

'Your Majesty, I must forbid it.'

'What would you have me do, Chancellor? Stay here in safety and be a puppet Queen for Commander Azaxyr. Stand by while my people are made slaves?'

Ortron bowed his head. 'Your Majesty puts me to shame.' He turned to Sarah. 'The Queen and I will join in your escape.'

'We need a diversion.' said Sarah. 'Your Majesty, do you think you could manage a really convincing faint?'

They made their preparations, and sent a nervous Alpha Centauri to Sskel, who stood just outside the door. 'Come quickly, the Queen is ill! You must summon assistance.'

Sskel lumbered into the room. Queen Thalira lay slumped on the throne apparently unconscious.

Unnoticed, Alpha Centauri scuttled out of the door.

Sskel leaned over the throne, studying the unconscious Queen more closely. He was already off balance when Ortron and Sarah sprang at him combining their strength in an enormous shove. Sskel staggered and almost fell, clutching at the high back of the throne for support.

'Run, everyone,' yelled Sarah, and sprinted through the door, after Alpha Centauri.

Ortron ran after her. Thalira made to follow, but found she couldn't move. One of Sskel's enormous feet was planted firmly on the long train of her dress.

Ortron turned in the doorway, saw what was happening and ran back to help her, throwing himself on Sskel. With a sweep of one mighty arm Sskel sent Ortron reeling—but his foot moved as he did so, and Thalira's dress came free.

Ortron struggled to his feet. 'Run Your Majesty!'

Awkward in the long dress, Thalira ran for the door.

Sskel raised his sonic gun, taking aim at the retreating figure. He fired—just as Ortron threw himself in front of the gun. Ortron twisted in the sonic blast, and fell dead to the ground. Abandoning all thought of escape, Thalira turned back, and threw herself beside his body. 'No, Ortron, no,' she sobbed. But the Chancellor was dead.

A shadow fell over her, and she looked up to see Sskel standing above her, his sonic gun aimed at her head.

Thalira closed her eyes—and a voice from the doorway hissed, 'No, Sskel!'

Thalira opened her eyes and looked up. Azaxyr was standing in the doorway.

Obediently Sskel lowered his gun.

Azaxyr stalked forward. 'Where are the others?'

'They went to the mines, to join Gebek and the rebels,' said Thalira quickly. Perhaps the lie would buy Sarah and Alpha Centauri a little time.

'How very stupid of them. Let there be no more of this foolishness, Your Majesty.' He glanced down at Ortron's body. 'You have seen the results of opposition. Guard her Sskel!'

Flattening themselves in an alcove of rock, Gebek and the Doctor waited for an Ice Warrior to pass by. The great helmet-like head swung to and fro, suspiciously, and for a moment they thought it had seen them. But it moved on at last, and the Doctor and Gebek were just about to head for the refinery, when they heard more heavy footsteps.

It was Azaxyr, attended by an Ice Warrior guard.

The two massive figures passed down the tunnel and through the refinery door.

Inside the refinery was a small control room, crammed on all four sides with instrument banks. The massive figures of Azaxyr and his escort seemed to fill the little room, towering over Eckersley, who was checking an instrument panel in the corner.

'Ah, Eckersley, my friend,' said Azaxyr. 'It is good to see you. Have you shut off the ventilation system?'

'Yes. The miners will be getting very short of air by now.'

'Excellent. The Queen has made a foolish attempt to escape me—an attempt which Chancellor Ortron did not survive. The Ambassador and the Doctor's assistant have taken refuge in the mines.'

The Doctor and Gebek were flattened against the wall, just to one side of the still-open refinery door, close enough to overhear the conversation. The Doctor was listening in mounting astonishment. He could understand Eckersley's policy of non-involvement, even though he didn't approve of it. But why was Azaxyr being so cordial to the engineer? It was almost as if they were old friends . . .

Alpha Centauri hovered nervously over the control panel in the communications room, watched impatiently by Sarah. 'Come on,' she urged. 'We may not have much time.'

'I am trying to remember the correct sequence of instructions.'

'Well, hurry!'

'Sarah, you are making me nervous!'

'All right, sorry. I'll leave you to get on with it.' Sarah wandered over to the monitor consoles and began flicking pictures up on the screens. After a boring sequence of pictures of empty mine galleries, she suddenly found herself looking at Azaxyr and Eckersley in the refinery.

Alpha Centauri remembered the correct coding sequence at last, and a light began pulsing regularly on his console, a sign that the emergency signal was being transmitted.

He moved over to Sarah. 'It is done. Though, of course, there is no guarantee that the Federation will receive it, or act upon it if they do.'

'Take a look at this,' said Sarah. 'Eckersley and Azaxyr. They look very chummy.'

'Chummy?'

'Friendly—as if they were working together. Can you get me sound on this thing?'

Alpha Centauri snaked out a tentacle and adjusted controls. Suddenly they heard Azaxyr's voice. 'I see no reason for you to continue this masquerade, Eckersley. Why not join me openly?'

Then Eckersley said, 'Oh no. We agreed, remember, I stay undercover until your plan's succeeded.'

'But it has—the planet is almost ours.'

'Almost isn't good enough, Commander. Things could still go wrong, and if they do—well, I'm just the innocent bystander.'

'As you wish. But as soon as we begin shipping the trisilicate to Galaxy Five, you need worry no longer.'

Alpha Centauri stared at Sarah in horror. 'They are *both* traitors to the Federation!'

They heard Eckersley's voice. 'They've agreed our terms?'

'Subject to a time-limit Eckersley. Without the trisilicate, Galaxy Five cannot continue the war much longer. We must conclude matters quickly.'

Like Alpha Centauri and Sarah, the Doctor was listening to this conversation in horrified fascination. He edged closer to the door.

In the refinery, Eckersley was saying, 'Well, I'm ready to start refining. How soon can you regain control of the mines?'

'It will not be easy. The miners are obstinate.'

'They'll have to come up when the air gets unbreathable.'

'That will take time—and time is short!'

Eckersley laughed. 'I know—we'll winkle them out with good old Aggedor.' He pulled back a plastic curtain to reveal a separate control console. Standing on top of it was a statue of Aggedor, a smaller version of the one in the temple. Eckersley began operating the controls, and a picture of one of the mine galleries appeared on a built-in monitor screen. 'One or two Aggedor manifestations will get 'em on the move!' He flicked up more pictures on the scanner. 'Ah, here we are!' The monitor showed four miners in a gallery . . .

The four miners moved wearily along the gallery. They were survivors of the battle with the Ice Warriors; they had taken refuge in the lower galleries, until driven to the surface by the increasingly foul air. Now they were hoping to escape from the mines into the open air—if the Ice Warriors didn't find them first.

Suddenly a fiercely glowing shape appeared on the rock wall ahead of them—a snarling image of Aggedor, the angry roar of the monster filled the gallery. 'It is Aggedor,' screamed one of the miners. 'It is the spirit of Aggedor!'

They turned and ran, all but one, who stood frozen in terror. He turned to follow the others, but he was too late. A fierce ray of light shot from the image—the miner's body glowed brightly, and then disappeared.

The three surviving miners raced on in terror. The spirit of Aggedor had claimed another sacrifice.

10

Trapped in the Refinery

'It seems the Doctor was right,' said Alpha Centauri.
'The appearances of Aggedor are technological trickery—controlled by Eckersley. Why has he been doing
this?'

'It's pretty obvious, isn't it?' said Sarah. 'He was
deliberately making things worse, so he could persuade
you to send for his Ice Warrior friends. Look Ambassador! Look!'

Alpha Centauri looked. The scene on the monitor
showed the open refinery door, over the shoulders of
Eckersley, Azaxyr and his guard, who were all facing the
other way. A very familiar face was peering round the
edge of that door.

'It's the Doctor!' cried Sarah joyfully. 'He's alive!
He's alive after all. You stay here, Ambassador, see if
you can boost that distress call. I'm lting to join the
Doctor.'

Alpha Centauri looked at the monitor screen. There
was no doubt about it, he thought—the Doctor had an
extraordinary capacity for survival!

The voice of one of Azaxyr's sub-commanders came
from the communicator on his wrist. 'The miners are
fleeing in terror from the lower levels. We are destroying
them as they emerge.'

Azaxyr spoke into the wrist-unit. 'See that as many exits as possible are covered. They must not escape.' He had already decided that it would be simpler to exterminate the rebellious miners and replace them with imported technicians using modern machinery. He lowered the communicator. 'It seems your plan is working, Eckersley.'

'Then I'd better keep up the good work,' said Eckersley cheerfully. It did not bother him in the least that he was driving the miners to their deaths under the sonic guns of the waiting Ice Warriors. It was all in the way of business.

All along the galleries, miners fled in terror before the angry spirit of Aggedor—fled to the upper exits, and the waiting guns of the Ice Warriors.

'What's happening, Doctor?' whispered Gebek.

'Eckersley's summoning up his fake Aggedor to frighten your people out of the mines.'

'We've got to stop him!'

The Doctor shook his head. 'If we show ourselves now, Azaxyr will kill us on sight. We'll have to wait our chance.'

Eckersley looked up from his machine. 'Projector's overheating a bit. We can always give them another dose later.'

'Excellent! Let us return to the Citadel!'

Azaxyr led the way out of the refinery, followed by his guard, and Eckersley followed.

As Eckersley locked the door, Azaxyr said, 'Can you reset the alarm system?'

Eckersley examined the control panel and shook his

head. 'Not from here. The late-lamented Doctor seems to have jiggered the sub-control circuits. I'll have to use the master control circuit from the communications room.'

'Let us go there at once,' Azaxyr turned to his Ice Warrior. 'You will stay here and guard the refinery.'

Azaxyr and Eckersley moved away, leaving the Ice Warrior standing sentry outside the refinery doors.

The Doctor and Gebek flattened themselves against the archway as they passed by. 'How long will it take them to get back to the Citadel from here?' whispered the Doctor.

'Five minutes, maybe ten, why?'

'That's how long we've got to dispose of our Ice Warrior friend there and get into the refinery.'

'How?' asked Gebek. 'He'll blast us down as soon as we break cover.'

'What we need is a distraction,' said the Doctor. He listened. 'And I think I hear one coming.'

Sarah came dashing down the side tunnel, going so fast that she ran straight past the patrolling Ice Warrior before he could stop her.

The Ice Warrior swung round, raising its sonic gun. 'Stop! Stay where you are!'

Behind the archway, the Doctor pointed down at their feet to a huge chunk of loose rock. He and Gebek lifted it between them and rushed towards the Ice Warrior, whose back was now towards them. Before it could turn, they brought the great boulder smashing down on its head. The Ice Warrior crashed to the ground, like a cut-down tree.

Sarah rushed up to the Doctor and hugged him. 'I thought you'd been blown up in the cave.'

'No, that was poor old Ettis.'

'Can't you ever stay out of trouble?'

'My dear Sarah, there's nothing I like better than a quiet life.' Gently the Doctor disentangled himself.

102

'Now, I've got a very complicated job to do in a very short time. Come on, Gebek, we'd better get the body out of sight.' Between them they dragged the body of the Ice Warrior into a side tunnel, and covered it with rubble. A few minutes later, the Doctor was at work on the lock of the refinery door with his sonic screwdriver.

Alpha Centauri jumped nervously back from the console as Azaxyr and Eckersley came into the communications room.

Azaxyr looked at him in surprise. 'Ambassador! What are you doing here? I was informed that you had joined forces with the rebels in the mines.'

'Nonsense,' said Alpha Centauri. 'I was merely trying to keep out of the way.'

Azaxyr looked thoughtfully at him. 'But why here, in the communications room. Why not in your own quarters? Could it be that you have been trying to send a message to the Federation?'

Suddenly he spotted the flashing light on the console. 'The distress beacon! You have been very foolish, Ambassador!'

'I merely thought that since things were getting out of control it would be wise to summon help for you.'

'Things are not out of control,' hissed Azaxyr angrily. 'This planet will soon be under my command. Disobey me again, and you will suffer the consequences.' He raised his sonic gun threateningly.

Terrified Alpha Centauri backed away, and Eckersley said, 'I'm sure the Ambassador meant it for the best.'

Azaxyr considered, and then lowered the sonic gun. 'Very well. I shall give you another chance, Ambassador. You will accompany me to the throne room.' He went out, and Eckersley and Alpha Centauri followed.

Outside the communications room, Eckersley said,

'I'll catch you up—I forgot to switch on the refinery alarms.'

He went back into the communications room.

'Got it!' said the Doctor at last, and the refinery door swung open. He ushered Sarah and Gebek inside and followed them, closing the door behind him, just as—

Eckersley in the communications room, pressed the master switch that reactivated the refinery alarms.

In the throne room, Azaxyr towered over Queen Thalira, who sat huddled and terrified on her throne. 'Trisilicate production will be resumed immediately, using all available modern machinery. I shall expect your help, Your Majesty, in obtaining the full co-operation of your people.'

'When my father signed the treaty with the Federation, he could not have known that it would bring us nothing but bloodshed. Now I suppose we must endure the consequences.'

The slur on the Federation was too much for Alpha Centauri. 'Do not believe him Your Majesty. The Federation has had no part in all this slaughter. Commander Azaxyr is a traitor and a renegade. Eckersley also! They plan to betray the Federation and ship the trisilicate to our enemies of Galaxy Five.'

With a hiss of rage, Azaxyr raised his sonic gun. 'You were warned, Ambassador!'

Just as he was about to fire, Eckersley shouted, 'No, Commander. What does it matter what he knows. He's a Federation Ambassador—he could still make a useful hostage.'

'Thank you, Eckersley,' said Alpha Centauri. His

indignation overcame him. 'But you are still a renegade and a traitor!'

'Is what the Ambassador says true?' asked Queen Thalira. 'Is Commander Azaxyr really acting without Federation authority?'

'It's true, right enough. What difference does it make to you?'

'A great deal,' said Queen Thalira indignantly. 'Our loyalty is due only to the Federation—and Peladon has never dishonoured a treaty.'

Azaxyr pointed dramatically to the towering Ice Warrior in the doorway. 'There is your only loyalty—you will obey or perish.'

Eckersley looked almost admiringly at Alpha Centauri. 'You must be a lot brighter than you look, Ambassador. How come you're so well-informed?'

'You were betrayed by your own security system, Eckersley. When you were conspiring with the Commander, Sarah and I overheard you on the monitor . . .'

Azaxyr swung round on him. 'Sarah? You said she was with the rebels in the mines. Where is she?' The gun came up again. 'Answer if you value your life.'

Terrified Alpha Centauri babbled, 'She went to join the Doctor in the refinery . . .'

'The Doctor in the refinery!' Azaxyr turned to Sskel. 'You will go to the refinery at once. If the Doctor is there—destroy him.'

The Doctor was busy at the controls of the ventilation system. 'The first thing to do is to give those miners of yours some air—there that should do it!'

Sarah had found the statue of Aggedor in the alcove. 'Look at this, Doctor.'

'Yes, I know. A simple holographic projector, linked to a directional heat-ray. The projector transmits a giant image of Aggedor, and the heat-ray does the damage.'

Sarah shivered. 'Instant Aggedor—complete with fiery breath!'

'The appearances that terrified my people,' said Gebek. 'They were all done from here?'

'That's right. By Eckersley, or his Ice Warrior friend.' The Doctor looked almost admiringly at the machine. 'A very clever piece of work, this.' Fascinated as always, by a new piece of scientific gadgetry, the Doctor studied the controls absorbedly.

No one noticed the blank eyes of Sskel staring through the plasti-glass window set in the door.

Outside Sskel tried the door gently, and then raised his wrist communicator. 'The Doctor is in the refinery, but the door is locked. Send help.' Sskel raised his sonic gun and fired at the lock.

'I think I've got the hang of it,' said the Doctor. 'The directional co-ordinates are here, you see, and the heat-ray . . .'

Sarah sniffed, looked round the room, and pointed to the door. 'Look!'

The Doctor and Gebek looked.

A whisp of smoke was coming from the lock.

Two more Ice Warriors lumbered down the tunnel. Sskel stepped back, and indicated the refinery door. 'Help me!'

All three Ice Warriors raised their guns and opened fire. The door twisted and buckled beneath the energy-impact of the sonic guns.

'What puzzles me is this, Eckersley,' said Alpha Centauri severely. 'What is the reason for your betrayal?'

'Money,' said Eckersley simply. 'A simple matter of business. I get a percentage of all the trisilicate mined on

Peladon—enough to make me one of the richest men in the galaxy. And that's just for starters, later there'll be power as well.'

'Power?'

'When Galaxy Five win this war, their helpers will be well rewarded. Maybe they'll make me ruler of Earth!'

'And what of Commander Azaxyr? What are his motives?'

'A certain number of die-hard Ice Warriors didn't like it when Mars decided to join the Federation. Azaxyr's head of a kind of breakaway group. They want a return to the good old days of military conquest, death or glory.' He looked up as Azaxyr came over to them. 'Ah, Commander, we were just talking about you!'

'I have received a message from Sskel,' hissed Azaxyr triumphantly. 'It appears that the Doctor is indeed alive—but not for long. Sskel has him trapped in the refinery.'

The Doctor was working frantically at the controls of the holographic projector.

Sarah looked at the door, which was visibly buckling under the combined attack of the Ice Warriors. 'Doctor, can't you stop playing with that thing and do something?'

'I am doing something, Sarah. But at this close range the co-ordinates are very tricky . . .'

Sarah peered through the plasti-glass at the three huge shapes looming outside the door. 'Do hurry, Doctor. There's a whole gang of them out there now!'

Gebek said, 'The door won't hold much longer, Doctor. They'll be through in a minute.'

The Doctor shot a hurried glance at the door. Its whole surface was buckling inwards, and streams of molten metal were running down from the lock.

Gebek was right. There were only minutes to go . . .

11

The Threat

'Right!' said the Doctor. 'Here we go! Keep your fingers crossed everybody.' He threw a switch.

A glowing image of Aggedor materialised on the rock wall behind the three Ice Warriors. Ponderously they swung round. The sight of Aggedor struck no terror to their hearts—but Eckersley had equipped his fake monster with a weapon that was the Ice Warriors' greatest enemy—heat!

As they staggered back from the glowing radiance, the heat-ray shot out, killing the nearest Ice Warrior instantly. Sskel and the other Ice Warriors turned to flee. The ray shot forth again, killing the second Ice Warrior. With a surprising turn of speed, Sskel lumbered through the archway and disappeared down the tunnel.

Sarah peered through the little window. 'You've done it, Doctor. They've gone!'

The Doctor patted the projector. 'We've got a chance to win now, Gebek, but we'll have to act quickly. Go back to the mines and rally your men.'

'It won't be easy, Doctor. Their spirit has gone. So many of them have been killed . . . Now they think Aggedor has turned against them . . .'

'Then we must convince them differently.'

'How?'

'Perfectly simple, my dear chap. We arrange the time

and place between us, and when you've got them all together . . .'

Sskel lurched into the throne room, Azaxyr swung round, sensing something had gone wrong. 'Has the Doctor been destroyed?'

'No, Commander,' gasped Sskel. 'He is in the refinery.'

'The Doctor is still alive? What happened?'

'He used Aggedor as a weapon against us.'

'Send more warriors!'

'It is useless, Commander. We cannot approach the area. The heat from the Aggedor projection will destroy us.'

Eckersley came forward. 'Don't worry, Commander, I'll winkle him out. I built that refinery—it's still got one or two tricks the Doctor doesn't know about.'

'I shall accompany you to the communications room. Sskel—you will remain here and guard Her Majesty and the Ambassador.'

Alpha Centauri and Thalira exchanged worried glances—but with Sskel looming over them, there was nothing they could do.

At a junction not far from the refinery, Gebek was addressing a small dispirited group of miners.

'How can we fight on, Gebek,' asked one of them wearily. 'Aggedor has turned against us . . .'

'No,' snapped Gebek. 'You are wrong!'

'Aggedor slew many of us, and drove the rest of the guns of Azaxyr's warriors.'

'That was trickery, employed by our enemies. Aggedor fights for us, protects the men of Peladon as he has always done.'

There was a dispirited murmur.

'You do not believe me?' shouted Gebek. 'Look!' He pointed dramatically to a spot on the gallery wall. Nothing happened.

'Come on, Doctor,' growled Gebek beneath his breath. 'Now!'

The Doctor registered Gebek's dramatic gesture on the projector's monitor screen. 'Right,' he said to himself, and operated controls.

'Well, Gebek,' growled one of the miners. 'What are we waiting for?'

To Gebek's relief, a glowing spot appeared on the tunnel wall. It grew rapidly into a glowing image of Aggedor.

'Do not fear, brothers,' shouted Gebek. 'Aggedor will not harm us, he will slay only our enemies.' He walked boldly towards the image stretching out his arms. 'Aid us, O Aggedor!'

There was a single fierce roar, and Aggedor faded away. Gebek turned back to the miners. 'Well—now will you fight?'

Eckersley and Azaxyr were observing the scene on the communications room monitor. 'Looks pretty tricky, doesn't it?'

'My warriors will soon destroy these primitives,' hissed Azaxyr.

'Not if these primitives have got my Aggedor's heat-ray helping them. Time for a word with the Doctor, I think.'

'There's no doubt about it,' said the Doctor. 'Eckersley worked it all out very well.'

110

'Thanks for the compliment, Doctor!'

It was Eckersley's voice, coming from some hidden speaker.

'He must be in the communications room,' whispered Sarah.

'That's right, love. You can't see me, but I can see you.'

'Then you'll know that I have control of Aggedor,' said the Doctor. 'Tell you what, why don't you just surrender right away?'

They heard Eckersley laugh, 'You know, Doctor, I admire you, I really do. But you're the one who's going to surrender.'

'What's he talking about?' asked Sarah.

'Just bluffing, Sarah.'

'Oh no I'm not,' said the unseen Eckersley. 'Remember my little security system, love? It works inside as well as out!'

The discordant shrieking of the alarm noise filled the air, and the dizzying light pattern began flashing all around them.

'That's just the lowest level, Doctor,' said Eckersley's triumphant voice. 'Will you come out and surrender, or do I have to step it up?'

The Doctor leaned towards Sarah, his lips to her ear. 'Sarah, you'd better get out of here. Find Gebek, and warn him they'll be waiting for him. I'll try and help with Aggedor.'

'What about you?'

'This kind of nonsense doesn't bother me. Now, off you go, there's not much time.'

Eckersley turned to Azaxayr and said confidently, 'They won't be able to stand much more of that—especially if I step it up!'

'Excellent!' hissed Azaxyr. 'I will go and set an

ambush with my warriors!'

As Azaxyr left, Eckersley spoke into the microphone. 'Well, Doctor, have some sense. Clear off now. Believe it or not, I don't want to hurt you. Surrender now, and I'll do my best to persuade Azaxyr to let you go. He won't care about you two once he's in control of the planet.'

The Doctor's voice came back. 'Sorry, old chap, can't chat now, I'm rather busy.'

'Obstinate old devil,' muttered Eckersley, and reached for the alarm system controls.

In the refinery the light and sound effects began to increase. The air was filled with unbearable noises, dazzling lights.

Gritting his teeth the Doctor tried to shut them from his consciousness. He was hunched over the projector, tracking Gebek and his miners through the tunnels. They would run into Azaxyr's ambush soon . . . and if he wasn't able to help them . . .

Gebek's force was growing minute by minute, as word spread through the mines that Aggedor was once more fighting for his people.

Suddenly the little army ran into a strong force of Ice Warriors, the advance guard of Azaxyr's troops.

The miners scattered, and ducked back into hiding.

'Do not flee, brothers,' roared Gebek. 'Aggedor fights with us!'

There was an angry roar and the glowing image of Aggedor appeared on the rock wall. The heat-ray shot forth, killing the nearest Ice Warrior instantly.

'Aggedor fights with us,' shouted Gebek again.

With a roar of triumph, the miners rushed forward, driving the Ice Warriors before them.

Again and again, the image of Aggedor appeared, destroying their enemies with his fiery breath.

Azaxyr stormed into the communications room. 'What is happening, Eckersley? The Doctor is still using Aggedor to attack us in the mines. My warriors are being destroyed. You must stop him!'

Eckersley leaned over the speaker. 'Last chance, Doctor. Surrender now, or I'll turn the alarms to maximum. Your brain will be totally destroyed.'

On the monitor they could see the Doctor hunched over the projector. He made no reply.

Almost reluctantly, Eckersley turned the controls to maximum power.

'He is still resisting,' hissed Azaxyr.

'Not for much longer,' said Eckersley confidently. 'He'll keel over any minute now.'

Sskel lumbered into the room. 'Commander Azaxyr, the miners have almost reached the Citadel.'

'We shall prepare an ambush for them,' announced Azaxyr. 'Eckersley, you will deal with the Doctor!'

The combined effect of the noise and lights in the refinery was almost unbearable now.

The Doctor leaned groggily over the projector, tracking Gebek and his men on the monitor. They had almost reached the Citadel by now—this was the last, most vital stage of the attack. He *had* to hang on . . .

In the corridor outside the secret passage to the mines, Azaxyr was preparing for the final struggle, placing his few remaining warriors in ambush. 'Remember,' he hissed, 'this is our last chance for victory.'

In the secret passage, Gebek was readying his men for the final attack. 'Our first task is to see that the Queen is safe, then the Ambassador. Then we will deal with Azaxyr, and the Federation troops. Remember, Aggedor is with us!'

The secret door swung open, and Gebek and his advance guard moved forward. Suddenly there was the crackle of sonic guns. Caught in a crossfire, Gebek's men were falling all around us.

'Help us, Aggedor!' someone screamed. But Aggedor did not appear.

In the refinery, the scene on the projector monitor swam before the Doctor's eyes. Gebek's men were being shot down. He had to manage one final manifestation. Summoning up the last reserves of his concentration, he adjusted the projector controls.

A fierce heat beat on the backs of Azaxyr's Ice Warriors. Aggedor had materialised behind them. One by one they fell before the deadly heat-ray, until only a handful were left alive. Abandoning his troops, Azaxyr headed for the throne room. Now there was just one card left to play.

Another Ice Warrior died beneath Aggedor's fiery ray. Aggedor faded and did not reappear. By now, it didn't matter. Gebek's men were unstoppable.

Overwhelming the last few Ice Warriors by sheer weight of numbers, they swept on towards the throne room.

Caught up in the wake of the triumphant little army, Sarah ran into the Citadel. Pausing to snatch up a blaster, from beside the body of a dead miner, she headed for the communications room.

Eckersley watched the Doctor slump forward over the console, and slide slowly to the ground. 'Got you, Doctor!'

A voice behind him said, 'Turn it off.'

Eckersley turned round and saw Sarah in the door-way, covering him with a blaster. 'You wouldn't use that,' he said easily.

'Wouldn't I?' said Sarah. 'Turn off that alarm—now!' She raised the blaster.

Eckersley took another look at her face and said hastily. 'Okay, okay!' He went over to the alarm console and switched off the power. 'It's served its purpose anyway. Your friend the Doctor's dead.'

'I don't believe you!'

'Take a look for yourself then.'

Eckersley stepped aside, and Sarah came over to look at the monitor.

She saw the Doctor's body on the refinery floor, gave a gasp of horror—and Eckersley jumped her, taking away her gun. She stepped back as he raised the blaster to cover her.

'I had a nice little scheme going until you and your friend the Doctor turned up,' said Eckersley bitterly. 'I ought to . . .' He raised the blaster.

Sarah looked steadily at him.

'Turn around,' he ordered. 'Hands up!'

Sarah obeyed.

She heard the communications room door close, and spun round. Eckersley was gone.

She ran to the door and tried to open it, but it was locked. She went back to the monitor, and looked sadly at the motionless body of the Doctor.

Eckersley hurried down the corridor, and ran into a straggler from Gebek's army.

Sword in hand, the miner barred his way. 'Engineer

115

Eckersley, Gebek has given orders for your capture.'

'Oh, get out of my way,' said Eckersley impatiently.

'You are my prisoner,' announced the miner importantly.

Eckersley might not be up to shooting young girls down in cold blood, but he was quite prepared to kill where his own safety was threatened. 'Sorry, chum, I've got too much to do.'

The miner advanced threateningly, raising his sword.

Eckersley raised his blaster, shot the man down, stepped over the body and hurried on his way.

Gebek and his men burst into the throne room—to find Azaxyr and Sskel standing by the throne, looming over Queen Thalira and a terrified Alpha Centauri.

Azaxyr's sonic gun was aimed directly at Queen Thalira's head. 'Surrender, Gebek,' he hissed. 'Tell your men to lay down their arms—or the Queen will die!'

12

Aggedor's Sacrifice

For a moment nobody moved

Then Gebek said evenly, 'We have no choice—there is only one thing we can do.'

He nodded to the nearest miner, a massive figure as brawny as Gebek himself.

Gebek hurled himself at Azaxyr, and the miner threw himself on Sskel . . . who instantly shot him down.

Gebek knew he had no hope of overcoming Azaxyr—his one aim was to deflect Azaxyr's gun arm from Queen Thalira's head. Wrapping both arms around Azaxyr's one, Gebek wrenched it down with all his strength.

Sskel aimed his sonic gun at the struggling pair, not daring to shoot for fear of hitting his Commander.

Gebek swung Azaxyr's arm around and the sonic gun fired—at the precise moment it was pointing at Sskel.

The giant Ice Warrior staggered back, firing his own gun as if by reflex. The sonic blast smashed into Azaxyr's body at close range, killing him instantly.

The miners watched unbelievingly, as first Sskel and then Azaxyr toppled and fell, crashing to the ground like fallen trees.

Gebek ran to the throne.

'Are you all right, Your Majesty?'

'I am safe, thank you, Gebek.'

She called to Alpha Centauri, who was standing

beside the throne quivering, his tentacles wrapped over his single eye. 'Ambassador!'

Alpha Centauri opened his eyes, astonished to find himself alive. 'Yes, Your Majesty?'

'I think you should contact the Federation, and inform them of the situation here.'

Alpha Centauri looked down at the fallen bodies and shuddered. 'The late Commander Azaxyr's ship was jamming the signals, Your Majesty.'

'Nevertheless, you must try!'

'At once, Your Majesty.'

Alpha Centauri hurried to the communications room, unlocked the door and was surprised to find a disconsolate Sarah. 'I wondered what hae happened to you, Sarah. There is good news. The Ice Warriors are defeated, and Azaxyr is dead.'

'So is the Doctor,' said Sarah flatly. 'Eckersley killed him.'

'Eckersley? The Doctor dead? Are you sure?'

Sarah pointed towards the monitor. 'See for yourself. He's in the refinery. I'm going down to him.'

Sarah left, and Alpha Centauri stared incredulously into the monitor.

Sadly he turned away. He tried the Federation communications circuit, and found that the jamming had ceased. (The crew of Azaxyr's ship had been monitoring the battle on their scanners. Gathering their Commander had been defeated, they had prudently taken themselves off.)

Alpha Centauri spoke into the communicator. 'This is Federation Ambassador on the planet Peladon. Connect me to the Security Council immediately—priority one! I have an urgent message.'

His message safely delivered, and with an assurance from a horrified Federation that help was on the way,

Alpha Centauri was back in the throne room, telling Thalira of Eckersley's part in the plot.

The Queen was shocked. 'I find it hard to believe that Eckersley could be so wicked.'

'He is totally ruthless, Your Majesty. We must not forget that he is still at large. He has nothing to lose now.'

'Quite right, Ambassador,' said a familiar voice. They looked up to see Eckersley facing them, blaster in hand. 'All right, Your Majesty, you're coming with me!'

Alpha Centauri was horrified. 'Eckersley—what is the purpose of this outrage?'

'I've got a space ship hidden away on the other side of the mountain; my emergency exit, in case things went wrong. Her Royal Highness here is going to be my safe conduct.'

'I insist that you surrender immediately, Eckersley. I shall summon assistance. Help, guards!'

Alpha Centauri staggered back as Eckersley's blaster thudded into the side of his head.

Slipping out of her heavy cloak, Thalira ran to the tapestry behind the throne and pulled it aside, revealing a door. She was about to open it when Eckersley shouted. 'Stop, or I fire.' He came over to her and grabbed her by the wrist. 'Where does this lead to?'

'There is a secret passage to the edge of the Citadel.'

'Couldn't be better,' said Eckersley. 'We'll go out this way.' He dragged her through the door, closing it behind them.

Sarah knelt by the Doctor's body. Tears welled up in her eyes, ran down her nose and splashed onto the Doctor's face. He opened one eye. 'Tears, Sarah Jane? Anyone would think you thought I was dead.'

'Well, of course I did,' said Sarah indignantly. 'You certainly *looked* dead!'

'Well, it was getting a bit noisy in here, you see. So when I couldn't stand the row from Eckersley's alarm system any longer, I went into a complete sensory withdrawal.'

'Into what?'

'A sort of trance. I switched myself off. It's an old Time Lord trick.'

'You mean you did it on purpose? And I had all that worry for nothing?'

'Don't sound so indignant, Sarah. Anyone would think you'd prefer me to be dead! Now then, let's go and find the others. What's been happening during my little nap?'

By the time they reached the throne room, Sarah had given the Doctor a full account of Gebek's victory.

As they entered, Gebek came rushing to meet them. 'Thank goodness you've come, Doctor. Eckersley has kidnapped the Queen.'

'What?'

Alpha Centauri was leaning against the throne, tentacles held to his aching head.

'Doctor! You are still alive.'

'Well, of course I'm alive. Now, tell me what's happened.'

Alpha Centauri gave a dramatic account of the kidnapping. When he had finished, the Doctor said, 'How well does Eckersley know these tunnels?'

'Better than anyone on Peladon,' said Alpha Centauri. 'He made a most thorough survey when he first came to this planet.'

'It won't be easy to find him, Doctor,' warned Gebek. 'I've got my men searching already, but this whole mountain is riddled with tunnels, some of them disused for years. And if Eckersley knows them all . . .'

'He's got a start on us too,' said Sarah. 'We could

search for days and never find him.'

The Doctor stood looking thoughtfully around the room. Suddenly he saw Thalira's abandoned cloak, draped across the throne. 'Don't worry, I think I know how we can track him down. Come on!' He snatched up the cloak.

'Where are we going?'

'To the temple of course. We're going to ask for Aggedor's help.'

Eckersely strode determinedly through the tunnels dragging Thalira behind him. He seemed to be completely sure of his route. They passed the scattered bodies of a group of miners killed in the battle.

'Look around you, Eckersley, ' said Thalira bitterly. 'Are you proud of what you have done?'

'Shut up and keep moving,' said Eckersley, and dragged her after him.

They hurried on and on weaving their way through a maze of tunnels, until even Eckersley was tired and needed to rest. He felt sure he was safe now—no one could have followed them over so complex a route. At a point where several tunnels joined, he let go of Thalira's arm, and she slumped tiredly against the wall.

Eckersley grinned mockingly at her. 'Bear up, Your Majesty, we're nearly there. My ship's not far off now.'

Ever cautious, Eckersley had hidden the little space ship in a concealed cleft in the mountain, using the sonic cannon to blast an access route. Soon he would be on his way to some remote planet, keeping well clear of Federation justice. There was always work for a good engineer somewhere in the galaxy.

'If your ship is near, then go to it,' said Thalira. 'Go, and leave me here. Peladon is well rid of you.'

'You're coming too, Your Majesty. I'll need you as a hostage until the last minute, just in case someone manages to follow me. Not that there's much chance of that!'

The Doctor's voice said, 'Don't be too sure, Eckersley!'

Eckersley turned to see the Doctor, Sarah, Gebek and a party of grim-faced miners.

'How did you find me?'

The Doctor stepped back, and an enormous furry form shuffled forwards.

'With the help of Aggedor! He's getting on a bit, but he can still sniff out a trail.' The Doctor held up the Queen's cloak, which was draped over his arm. His voice hardened. 'You'd better come with us, Eckersley. It's all over.'

'Is it?' snarled Eckersley. He grabbed Thalira, holding her in front of him as a shield.

In a most unqueenly fashion, Thalira twisted round and bit him hard on the hand.

Eckersley shoved her savagely against the rock wall, and Thalira gave a cry of pain.

There was a thunderous roar from Aggedor, and the great beast threw itself on Eckersley.

The two crashed down together. They heard a blood-curdling growl, a cry from Eckersley, the muffled thump of a blaster—then silence.

Cautiously the Doctor knelt to examine the two bodies. He looked up. 'Dead. Both of them.'

The Doctor rose and draped Thalira's cloak about her shoulders.

For a moment Queen Thalira, Gebek and the miners stood with bowed heads.

Aggedor had died nobly, sacrificing himself for the Queen. It was a fitting end for the Royal Beast of Peladon.

The Doctor and Sarah had been summoned for an audience with the Queen.

Recovered from her ordeal, dressed in full regalia, Thalira sat proudly upon her royal throne. 'Once again Peladon owes you a great debt, Doctor, just as in my father's time. I hope you will stay longer this time, so that we can show our gratitude.'

'I doubt if that will be possible, Your Majesty,' said the Doctor gently.

'But I shall need your help and advice, Doctor.'

Sarah said boldly, 'Your Majesty, you stood up to Chancellor Ortron, to Azaxyr and his Ice Warriors. You don't need anyone's help now.'

Thalira refused to give up easily. 'I shall need a new Chancellor, Doctor, and I had hoped that you—'

'I can tell you the very man for the job, Your Majesty,' said the Doctor hurriedly. 'Gebek!'

'We have great admiration for Gebek, and he has served us loyally—but he is only a miner.'

'It's the man that counts, Your Majesty,' said the Doctor gently. 'You can always give him a title if he needs one.'

Thalira said sadly, 'But it seems all that I can give you, Doctor, is my thanks.'

The Doctor bowed. 'I shall always be grateful for the honour you have offered me, Your Majesty. But believe me, Gebek is your man.'

At that moment Alpha Centauri and Gebek came into the throne room together. Alpha Centauri was in a state of great excitement. 'Your Majesty, Doctor, there is wonderful news. The war with Galaxy Five is over! I have just heard from Federation HQ. It seems that it was only the hope of obtaining Peladon's trisilicate that made them go on fighting. Once they learned that Azaxyr's scheme had failed, they became most anxious to negotiate a peace treaty.' Alpha Centauri was positively rubbing his tentacles with glee.

Gebek took the Doctor aside. 'That blue box you were asking about Doctor, we've found it for you. It's in the third gallery, just off the main cavern.'

'Thank you, Gebek,' whispered the Doctor. 'I think I'll just pop along and check that it's all right.'

Alpha Centauri was already in deep conversation with the Queen and Gebek went over to join them.

The Doctor caught Sarah's eye, and they slipped out of the throne room.

He had always hated goodbyes.

The Doctor threw open the TARDIS door with a sigh of relief. 'Come on, Sarah, in you go!'

Sarah paused, looking mischieviously at him. 'You're sure you don't want to stay, Doctor? I mean it's a good job, Chancellor. Permanent civil service post, a pension too, I shouldn't wonder. I'd hate to stand in the way of your career!'

'In!' said the Doctor firmly.

Sarah went inside. The Doctor followed, closing the door behind them.

A wheezing, groaning sound echoed through the tunnels of Peladon and the TARDIS dematerialised.

The Doctor and Sarah were on their way.

DOCTOR WHO

Δ	0426200969	Doctor Who and the Destiny of the Daleks	75p
Δ	0426108744	MALCOLM HULKE Doctor Who and the Dinosaur Invasion	75p
Δ	0426103726	Doctor Who and the Doomsday Weapon	85p
Δ	0426200063	TERRANCE DICKS Doctor Who and the Face of Evil	85p
Δ	0426112601	Doctor Who and the Genesis of The Daleks	75p
Δ	0426112792	Doctor Who and the Giant Robot	85p
Δ	0426115430	MALCOLM HULKE Doctor Who and the Green Death	75p
Δ	0426200330	TERRANCE DICKS Doctor Who and the Hand of Fear	75p
Δ	0426201310	Doctor Who and the Horns of Nimon	85p
Δ	0426200772	Doctor Who and the Image of The Fendahl	75p
Δ	0426200934	Doctor Who and the Invasion of Time	75p
Δ	0426200543	Doctor Who and the Invisible Enemy	75p
Δ	0426201256	PHILIP HINCHCLIFFE Doctor Who and the Keys of Marinus	85p

DOCTOR WHO

Δ	0426116828	Doctor Who and the Planet of Evil	75p
Δ	0426106555	Dr Who and the Planet of the Spiders	85p
Δ	0426201019	Doctor Who and the Power of Kroll	85p
Δ	0426116666	Doctor Who and the Pyramids of Mars	75p
Δ	0426116585	PHILIP HINCHCLIFFE Doctor Who and the Seeds of Doom	85p
	0426200675	TERRANCE DICKS The Adventures of K9 and other Mechanical Creatures (illus)	75p
	0426200950	Terry Nation's Dalek Special (illus)	95p
	0426114477	Doctor Who Monster Book (Colour illus)	50p
	0426200012	The Second Doctor Who Monster Book (Colour illus)	70p
	0426118421	Doctor Who Dinosaur Book (illus)	75p
	0426200020	Doctor Who Discovers Prehistoric Animals (NF) (illus)	75p
	0426200039	Doctor Who Discovers Space Travel (NF) (illus)	75p
	042620004?	Doctor Who Discovers Strange and Mysterious Creatures (NF) (illus)	75p
	042620008X	Doctor Who Discovers the Story of Early Man (NF) (illus)	75p
	0426200136	Doctor Who Discovers the Conquerors (NF) (illus)	75p
	0426116151	TERRANCE DICKS AND MALCOLM HULKE The Making of Doctor Who	95p

		IAN MARTER	
Δ	0426200497	Doctor Who and the Sontaren Experiment	60p
Δ	0426110331	MALCOLM HULKE Doctor Who and the Space War	85p
Δ	0426200993	TERRANCE DICKS Doctor Who and the Stones of Blood	75p
Δ	0426119738	TERRANCE DICKS Doctor Who and the Talons of Weng Chiang	75p
Δ	0426115007	Doctor Who and the Terror of the Autons	75p
Δ	0426200233	Doctor Who and the Time Warrior	75p
Δ	0426200233	GERRY DAVIS	
Δ	0426110765	Doctor Who and the Tomb of the Cybermen	75p
Δ	0426200683	TERRANCE DICKS Doctor Who and the Underworld	75p
Δ	0426200683	TERRANCE DICKS Doctor Who and the Web of Fear	75p
Δ	0426110412	TERRANCE DICKS Doctor Who and the Loch Ness Monster	85p
Δ	0426118936	PHILIP HINCHCLIFFE Doctor Who and the Masque of Mandragora	85p
Δ	0426116909	TERRANCE DICKS Doctor Who and the Mutants	75p
Δ	0426201302	Doctor Who and the Nightmare of Eden	85p
Δ	0426112520	Doctor Who and the Planet of the Daleks	75p

If you enjoyed this book and would like to have information sent to you about other TARGET titles, write to the address below.

You will also receive:
A FREE TARGET BADGE!
Based on the TARGET BOOKS symbol — see front cover of this book — this attractive three-colour badge, pinned to your blazer-lapel or jumper, will excite the interest and comment of all your friends!

and you will be further entitled to:
FREE ENTRY INTO THE TARGET DRAW!
All you have to do is cut off the coupon below, write on it your name and address in *block capitals,* and pin it to your letter. Twice a year, in June, and December, coupons will be drawn 'from the hat' and the winner will receive a complete year's set of TARGET books.

Write to:

TARGET BOOKS
44 Hill Street
London W1X 8LB

cut here

Full name . . . .

Address. . . . .

. . . .

. . . .

Age. . . . .

PLEASE ENCLOSE A SELF-ADDRESSED STAMPED ENVELOPE WITH YOUR COUPON!